CHILD'S PLAY

The Last Fool Series
Book One

BILL MYERS

An Amaris Media International Publication

CHILD'S PLAY
The Last Fool series – Book One
Copyright @2013
Bill Myers

Published by:
Amaris Media International
www.Amarismedia.com

in partnership with:
Christian Writers Guild Publishing
5525 N Union Blvd., Suite 101
Colorado Springs, CO 80919

Cover created by: Jun Ares
Interior created by: Jeff Gerke

Printed by: BethanyPress

Scripture quotations marked "KJV" are taken from the Holy Bible, King
James Version, Cambridge, 1769.

Scripture taken from the New King James Version®. Copyright © 1982 by
Thomas Nelson, Inc. Used by permission. All rights reserved.

Scripture quotations marked "NIV" are taken from HOLY BIBLE, NEW
INTERNATIONAL VERSION. Copyright © 1973, 1978, 1984 by
International Bible Society. Used by permission of Zondervan Publishing
House.

ISBN: 978-0-578-13219-8

Printed in the United States of America

PREVIOUS PRAISE FOR BILL MYERS

Blood of Heaven

"With the chill of a Robin Cooke techno-thriller and the spiritual depth of a C.S. Lewis allegory, this book is a fast-paced, action packed thriller."

ANGELA HUNT, NY TIMES BESTSELLING AUTHOR

"Enjoyable and provocative. I wish I'd thought of it!"

FRANK E. PERETTI, THIS PRESENT DARKNESS

ELI

"The always surprising Myers has written another clever and provocative tale."

BOOKLIST

"With this thrilling and ominous tale Myers continues to shine brightly in speculative fiction based upon Biblical truth. Highly recommended."

LIBRARY JOURNAL

"*Thought provoking and touching, this imaginative tale blends elements of science fiction with Christian theology.*"

LIBRARY JOURNAL

"*Myers strikes deep into the heart of eternal truth with this imaginative first book of the Soul Tracker series. Readers will be eager for more.*"

ROMANTIC TIMES MAGAZINE

Angel of Wrath

"*Bill Myers is a genius.*

LEE STANLEY, PRODUCER, GRIDIRON GANG

The God Hater

"*When one of the most creative minds I know gets the best idea he's ever had and turns it into a novel, it's fasten-your-seat-belt time. This one will be talked about for a long time.*"

JERRY B. JENKINS AUTHOR OF LEFT BEHIND

"An original masterpiece."

DR. KEVIN LEMAN, BESTSELLING AUTHOR

"If you enjoy white-knuckle, page-turning suspense, with a brilliant blend of cutting-edge apologetics, The God Hater will grab you for a long, long time."

BEVERLY LEWIS, NY TIMES BESTSELLING AUTHOR

"I've never seen a more powerful and timely illustration of the incarnation. Bill Myers has a way of making the Gospel accessible and relevant to readers of all ages. I highly recommend this book."

TERRI BLACKSTOCK, NY TIMES BESTSELLING AUTHOR

"A brilliant novel that feeds the mind and heart, The God Hater belongs at the top of your reading list."

ANGELA HUNT, NY TIMES BESTSELLING AUTHOR

"The God Hater is a rare combination that is both entertaining and spiritually provocative. It has a message of deep spiritual significance that is highly relevant for these times."

PAUL CEDAR, CHAIRMAN MISSION AMERICA COALITION

"Once again Myers takes us into imaginative and intriguing depths, making us feel, think and ponder all at the same time. Relevant and entertaining. The God Hater is not to be missed.

The Voice

"A crisp, express-train read featuring 3D characters, cinematic settings and action, and, as usual, a premise I wish I'd thought of. Succeeds splendidly! Two thumbs up!"

"Nonstop action and a brilliantly crafted young heroine will keep readers engaged as this adventure spins to its thought-provoking conclusion. This book explores the intriguing concept of God's power as not only the creator of the universe, but as its very essence."

"It's a real 'what if?' book with plenty of thrills...that will definitely create questions all the way to its thought-provoking finale. The success of Myers's stories is a sweet combination of a believable storyline, intense action, and brilliantly crafted, yet flawed characters."

DALE LEWIS, TITLETRAKK.COM

The Seeing

"Compels the reader to burn through the pages. Cliff-hangers abound and the stakes are raised higher and higher as the story progresses—intense, action-shocking twists!"

TITLETRAKK.COM

When the Last Leaf Falls

"A wonderful novella. Any parent will warm to the humorous reminiscences and the loving exasperation of this father for his strong-willed daughter... Compelling characters and fresh, vibrant anecdotes of one family's faith journey."

--PUBLISHERS WEEKLY

Imager Chronicles

Myers is our 21st Century C.S. Lewis.

LIGHT OF LIFE MAGAZINE

WARNING:
The following contains explicit religious content.
Reader's discretion advised.

"In the inner wine cellar I drank of my Beloved,
And when I traveled this entire valley,
I no longer knew anything,
and lost the herd I was following."

ST. JOHN OF THE CROSS

one

B
E
R
N
A
R
D

Before we get going you should probably know you really can't trust anything I'm going to say. Nothing. Zip. Sorry. If you haven't heard, I'm a loon, a nutcase, an entire side of fries short of a kid's meal. Come to think of it, I'm probably missing the burger, soda, and action figure, too.

Is that clear? I hope so 'cause I sure don't want you to be expecting too much.

Even though you might have heard the rumors, I have to tell you it was *not* the tattoo's fault—at least according to the salt and pepper shakers. And I'm not talking those boring, institutional salt and pepper shakers. No siree. I'm talking about the cool, donkey ones my old roommate bought in Puerto Rico and left behind. The ones whose accents are so thick you can barely understand them—especially when the coffee mugs start going. Those coffee mugs, I tell you, give them two cups of leaded and they get to jabbering all night.

But I digress—something I do a lot of, so please accept my apologies now before we get started. Max, my best friend and roomie, says it's because my mind is full of such fantastic thoughts, they just keep bubbling over and spilling onto each other. What a guy. You'll love Max. But we'll get to him in a few minutes.

The point is, and I'm sure I had one, our little pod of less than a dozen patients (Nelson would know the exact number) had already stood in the med line where Nurse Hardgrove served the hospital's holy sacraments, each dose carefully measured out according to our unique brand of craziness.

From there we headed to the cafeteria and breakfast, where we grabbed our green food trays, white plastic spoons and white forks (they don't trust us with knives, not even plastic ones) and moved along the counter, our white tennis shoes squeaking on the freshly waxed linoleum.

You'd like our place, Sisco Heights Mental Health Facility. You may have even seen us on the news. Lots of times the State brings people through to show off what a great place it is. I've lived here most of my thirty-five years and love it. You would too, I mean if you were, well, you know.

Anyways, I'd just entered the cafeteria line when I overheard the two-headed dragon that was tattooed on Darcy's forearm arguing with itself:

"Idiots," the head with one eye complained. "They got the AC cranked up too high again." He threw in a little shiver for dramatic effect.

The other head, the one with two eyes said, "It's the middle of June, fool, what did you expect?"

"I expect I'm going to fire up and add some heat to this place."

The second head sighed, "Please . . ."

"What you sayin'? We still got a few rights around here."

I could tell things were getting kind of tense between them so I glanced around to make sure it was safe before trying to calm things down. The two attendants, Biff

3

and Britt (or is it Britt and Biff? I can never keep them straight.) were leaning against opposite walls, doing a pretty good imitation of being awake. The others were scattered around the couple tables and already digging in—except for cute little Chloe. She reminds us all of Peter Pan. I mean if Peter Pan was Asian. And if he was a she. Anyway, Chloe was behind me trying to make up her mind whether to have the overcooked stewed prunes or the undercooked refried beans, which, for the record, looked and tasted about the same.

"I'm a tad curious," the second dragon head said. "How is it that you do that?"

"Do what?" his partner asked.

"Get your lips flapping so fast your brain just gives up and throws in the towel."

They kept going at it, getting louder and louder, until I lowered my head to Darcy's forearm and whispered, "Excuse me? Fellas?"

One-Eye looked up at me and sighed. "What you want, chubby boy?"

"You know what they think about disagreements around here."

"You tellin' us you're a Peace Monitor now?"

"No, of course not."

"Then take your crazy someplace else. How 'bout that nice little light switch over there? She's lookin' kinda lonely."

Of course I know sarcasm when I hear it, and for the briefest second I thought I should file a Hate Speech Complaint. But Darcy was a friend. Well, sort of.

"Duck!" Chloe shouted.

Of course, Chloe is as nuts as the rest of us, which meant I smiled at her politely before ignoring her completely.

"You remember the last time you fired up?" The second head was practically shouting. "How all them overhead sprinklers came on?"

"They disconnected them. 'Sides, it wouldn't have happened if you hadn't got our big butt in the way. Making me shoot around it totally ruined my sense of perspective."

"You're a two-dimensional character. You don't got perspective."

Darcy broke in. You can't miss her voice. It's smoke cured from years of cigarettes and, I imagine, lots of cigars. "What you doing, freak?"

I looked up to see her frowning down at me with those lovely, lavender-caked eyes, complete with missing eyebrows and bald head.

"Oh, sorry." I straightened up. "I was just, uh." I motioned to her arm, which I've got to admit, is way more muscular than mine. "Your dragons, what are their names again?"

"Listen, perv, I told you I catch you talking to my arm one more time and I'm doing some serious rearranging of your—"

"I wasn't talking to your arm," I blurted. "Honest. Besides, they started it."

"Let's go, Bernie."

I turned to look across a steaming pan of watery oatmeal or watery scrambled eggs, which also look and taste the same, and saw Winona. She's a volunteer food server from our pod who wears aluminum foil around her neck and wrists. She also has white, Einstein-like hair and an IQ to match.

"Certainly you are cognizant how nervous she becomes around men of the male persuasion?" She motioned to Darcy. "And your intimate discussion with her tattoos . . ." She shook her head. "On my planet, a verbal exchange with tattoos is the final step in consummating a physical relationship."

Without missing a beat, Darcy answered, "On my planet, it's the last step before sneaking into a perv's room and setting him on fire."

I looked at Darcy and swallowed nervously.

She looked at me and stared blankly.

As usual, the tattoos paid no attention. Instead, I heard One-Eye taking a deep, wheezing breath. I looked down and, just as I feared, he was filling up. The other head swore as he ducked under Darcy's elbow. It was pretty clear he was going to barbecue everything in sight . . . including Darcy, so there was only one thing I could do. I didn't mean to be fresh, but I reached over and covered Darcy's arm with both of my hands. Better to fry my hands than set the place on fire.

"Muwaff ma muf are mou moing?" One-Eye shouted.

"Get your perverted hands off me, you perv!" Darcy shouted.

A third voice chimed in. "Hey, Freak!"

It was Jamal. Jamal the Jihadist. Jamal the joy-killer. Jamal the purveyor of pain. He'd shown interest in Darcy the first moment she joined our pod. Not that she gave him the time of day, but that didn't stop Jamal. As far as he was concerned, she was his property, whether she cared to acknowledge it or not—and he had the broken nose and bruised ribs, courtesy of her martial arts training, to prove it.

She didn't exactly need his protection, which explained why, as I turned to him, seeing my lame little life pass before my lame little eyes, I felt the pain of Darcy's food tray smashing into my skull.

I should have listened to Chloe.

But that didn't stop Biff and Britt (or was it Britt and Biff?) from leaving the walls they'd been holding up. Even as I collapsed to the floor, slipping into unconsciousness, the two orderlies rushed in, Tasers firing like bug zappers at a bug convention. But not at sweet Darcy. For some reason, the guys weren't real fond of Jamal. I don't remember how many shots it took to put him down, or how many kicking boots it took to keep him there. I was too busy drifting into darkness, grateful that once again, I'd managed to save our home.

two

D
R

A
A
D
I
L

I pulled my satchel from the passenger seat and crawled out. The tiny employee parking lot was surrounded by woods and covered in cold, drizzly fog. I shut and locked the door, blaming the cramped, micro-hybrid for the ache in my hip and knees. For the thousandth time I dreamed of my sister's invitation to join her at the retirement village in Arizona with its dry air and sympathetic heat. But it was only a dream. I was too much Alpha male to put my brain out to pasture and watch my body turn to pudding and toothpicks. Though between the early morning chill and yesterday's reaming out by Division, it almost sounded appealing . . .

"Don't misunderstand us, Doctor, we all appreciate your sensitivity and we all are on your side."

Of course there had been no *us* or *we* in the glass-walled office of the Public Service building. Just the young man with a spattering of fresh acne across his cheekbones. He was a third my age and wore a suit twice my weekly pay. But I'd never signed up for the money. I had Navy retirement for that. I was here to give back to a country that had given so much to me.

"I'll grant you your rehabilitation numbers are high, but the Department has taken great care to outline specific responses to specific infractions."

"I understand," I said, "but some patients take more time. Some need a more personal approach to—"

"Our rules are not arbitrary, Doctor. They've been tested and approved by professionals with far more experience in the field than either you or I."

I resisted the urge to ask Junior how much field time he'd put in outside the office, not counting the golf games and squash courts. But with age comes wisdom. Instead, I chose to sit silently and count his latest crop of pink and white pustules . . . and call myself a coward the rest of the day and on into the night.

Now, just before dawn, I did my best not to limp as I crossed the parking lot and started up the fifty-six worn concrete steps leading to the equally worn three-story hospital. If there had been a handrail, it was long gone. Old timers said this part of the city was almost as good as before the Uprising.

"Almost as Good." It had become our mantra. Nearly half a century had passed since we'd quit tearing ourselves apart with the Religious Wars—kicked off by the half dozen dirty nukes simultaneously detonated in major population centers. Of course that was only the beginning. Retaliation led to retaliation, all the way down to the state and community level. Then came the economic collapse, along with a couple pandemics also courtesy of the conflict (think drug resistant smallpox and MARV in the hands of the devout). It had taken a long, long time to return to *almost as good.* Well, except for the heightened surveillance. For whatever reason, Uncle Sam always had money for that.

As I worked my way up the steps, my mind drifted back to yesterday's dressing-down. "Besides your own malpractice suit, you are no doubt aware that the victim's family is suing the Department for reckless endangerment."

I nodded.

"And now that the press has picked it up . . ." He let the phrase hang in the air. I didn't touch it. "We're simply left with no alternative than to put you on six-month probation."

I took a slow, steady breath. "And my patients?"

"Oh, don't misunderstand us, Doctor. You'll still make your rounds to the hospitals. But there will be no action or diagnosis on your part that we in the Department will not first review and approve."

In one sense, I suppose I was lucky. If there had been more psychiatrists with my education, let alone passion, I would have faced suspension. But I had the fancy initials after my name, and no one doubted my commitment to the cause. History would never repeat itself. Not on my watch.

Sometimes, to this day, I wake up in the morning, my heart racing, my sheets damp from memories of them pounding on my father's door in the middle of the night . . .

"Ibrahim! Ibrahim, come out!" It was Reverend Johnson. Over the months of building tension, he'd handed me several religious tracts. "You're too hand-some a lad to burn in hell," he would say.

Of course I always gave the pamphlets to Poppa who disposed of them, always with a prayer for Allah's vengeance to fall upon the infidel's head.

"Ibrahim!" More pounding. "We know you're in there."

"He is not here!" Momma cried. She threw a plead-ing look to Poppa, begging him to remain silent. But that was not how Poppa lived. Despite her pleas and her clinging, he threw open the door. They stormed in, five or six of them, cursing, shouting, accusing the men from our mosque of the slaughter of several Christian families—men, women, children. And, sadly, they were probably right. Though it could just have easily been in response to an attack the Christians launched, or the Jews, or even the Buddhists, Dharma bless their pacifist hearts. That's how ugly things had become. Though, in the years to follow, it was merely a prelude.

That night Momma covered my eyes as she screamed, begging for mercy. I remember the sound of scuffling, men yelling, someone shouting praises to Jesus as Poppa pleaded to Allah. I remember them dragging him out the door and Momma following them into the street, still screaming, still crying.

I raced after them onto the porch, unsure what to do, frozen in fear and guilt. I watched as they punched and kicked my father, the scene lit by a burning house across the street. I remember the bursts of gunfire one block over, the distant wail of police sirens. I remember Momma pleading for mercy as they loaded him into a car, until she was struck hard with the butt of a rifle, bloody teeth flying from her mouth like pink pearls.

Yes, I know all about the dangers of religion. And I've supported every law that has freed us from its tyranny—the fines and penalties for hate speech, the deportation of militants, the incarceration and re-education of hardliners—until gradually, over the last several decades, the monster had finally been defanged.

That's the primary purpose of the Department of Religious Affairs—not to outlaw religion. Other countries have tried that and have only succeeded in increasing religious fervor. No, our purpose is to remove the differences, any aspect that leads to separation, or the feelings of inferiority and superiority. And thanks to our dogged determination and brave legislators, we now have a state philosophy whose only goals are peace, reconciliation, and social harmony. That's what we've achieved, and that's what I've dedicated my so-called golden years to maintain.

I arrived at the top of the steps and took a moment to catch my breath. The fog, which had rolled in from the bay, stretched nearly to the tops of the trees. Although the hospital was in the middle of the city, on one of its highest hills, it was surrounded by just over an acre of woods.

I traipsed through the wet grass of a sloppily-manicured terrace to my office. It had its own separate entrance, though the room wasn't much bigger than a walk-in closet. I unlocked the door and was greeted by the familiar smell of dust and mildew. I snapped on the light and turned on the little wall heater.

Was there still resistance to the Department's efforts? Absolutely. But now we had the law on our side. Penalties were swift and substantial. And for those who tried to obey but couldn't? For the mentally or emotionally unstable? Well, that's where my division came in. Every major mental health facility in the state has a small ward, or pod, for those who struggle with such disorders. Men like . . . I opened my satchel and pulled out a file labeled: Maxwell Portenelli.

I opened the folder for a quick review. Not that I hadn't studied it before. But after yesterday's lecture, I'd leave no room for error. His daughter would be checking him in later this morning. Apparently he was a famous icon in the fashion world. Worth millions. But success did not come easily. According to family members, he was consumed with work, often putting in ninety hours a week, neglecting relationships, sometimes sleeping in his studio, and having no social life outside of business. Eventually the stress and demands took their toll. Two and a half weeks ago, on his fiftieth birthday, he experienced a psychotic break that left him incapacitated for nearly seventy-two hours. During that time he claimed to have been taken to heaven where he had a lengthy conversation with god.

The episode generated an extreme shift in personality with serious consequences—retrograde amnesia, including the inability to recognize any family member, manic behavior, bouts of extreme giddiness, and a complete disregard for the company he'd dedicated his entire life to building. There had been some talk about a private institution, but since his issue was religious in nature, that meant State involvement and his eventual assignment here at Sisco Heights.

And the trigger for such a break? A power lunch with select members of his board at a local Chinese restaurant. Eyewitnesses said it was intense, heated, and demanding—typical of most Portenelli meetings. There was no indication of any problem throughout the course of the two-hour lunch, until he opened his fortune cookie and read the fortune.

Almost immediately he began to tremble. Soon after, he closed his eyes and, despite the calls and shouts of others, he entered a catatonic state.

He was transported to Mercy General where he was tested and kept for observation. Seventy-two hours later, when he regained consciousness and it was established there was no physiological or neurological damage, he was released in the hopes of a full recovery.

At home, although thoughtful and polite with family and household staff, he did not recognize them. Nor did he display the slightest interest in returning to work. Instead, he became fixated upon his experience, wishing only to talk about god.

And what was the fortune that brought about such a dramatic change in character? It simply read:

> "You are my favorite child."
> God

I shook my head. Poor devil. To be at the height of his career and suffer such a breakdown. It was an unusual case, there was no doubt about it. But that's why we were here. Whether his recovery took weeks or months, I would be at his side to help and serve.

That is my purpose. And, if you will, that is my call.

three

S
A
F
F
R
O
N

Now, 'fore you get all white and judgy on me, let's get a couple things straight:

I do what it takes to survive. And if that gets your suburban, self-righteous, Fruit of the Looms in a bunch then you ain't got no clue what Max is about, so you might as well stop reading this thing right now.

Johnny Jackson is my man. And right or wrong, you stand by your man.

I know I said a couple things, but I ain't big on legalistics so here's one more. I'm gonna try to keep my language "PG," but if somethin' slips out and singe your holy ears, let me 'pologize now 'fore we get in the heat of battle.

So, here goes . . .

It was early Friday morning and JJ had the dope sickness real bad. It'd been almost eighteen hours since his last medicine and he was pulled up in a little ball and sweatin' like a pig in a sauna. Sweatin' while hurlin' at one end and diarrheain' at the other. We was in our camp, nestled under the 43B off ramp. Rush hour was just beginnin', but I still hear JJ pretty good.

"Saffron," he moans through chatterin' teeth—what's left of them since, before the smack, he liked his crystal.

"Right here, baby," I shout over the roar.

"I gots spiders crawlin' all over me."

"I know, baby."

"They in my bones."

"It just the sickness. You get through it. You done it before."

"I can't do it. Not this time." He wretched again but nothin' come up . . . one of the advantages of a low cal diet. When he's done he turns his head to me and groans, "We got nothin'?"

"I told you, they jumped me last night at the recyclin' center. Cleaned me out."

"Four dollars. I just needs four dollars to—"

"We ain't got forty cents."

He moans and pulls himself up a little tighter.

Course it hurt me seein' him like that, but like I said we been through this with him before. And me? I kicked once or twice. Ain't no picnic. But once I got clean I stayed clean. I'm pretty good shape now, 'cept for some occasional candy for the nose and my daily minimum requirement of fortified wine—everybody s'ppose to drink eight cups a somethin' a day. And despite the rigors demanded of a workin' mom—part-time dumpster diver, full-time recycler—I keep a pretty good camp. Not that I'd be makin' Better Homes and Garden, but for me, JJ, Brandylin, my thirteen-year-old, and Mariposa, our six-foot-two drag queen/nanny, it's home.

"Saffron . . ."

But we wasn't makin' ends meet and I know 'xactly what he wants. Not that I blame him. Not in his state. But we agreed . . . no more walkin' the stroll. Still, in his condition and economics the way they is, includin' those wonderful Cal Tran boys who keep runnin' us off and confiscatin' our goods, it don't look like we got much choice.

I throw a look to Brandylin. She a few feet from Mariposa who's snorin' like a chain saw. But she all snuggled up nice and tight and sleepin' like a little kitten. Outdoor life suits her jus' fine. I be sure to tell her 'ol man next time he come by with his latest whore tryin' to steal her again.

"Saf . . ."

I took a deep breath. "I know, baby. But nobody be wantin' my goodies this time a mornin'."

He lets out another moan, so low and pitiful it hurt my gut.

I can't take no more. I grab my water bottle and get up. Stayin' hunched over, I move along the narrow walkway with the overpass restin' on my back. 'Cause of our prime real estate, we get lots of visitors. I'm hopin' one of 'em left a cotton as a thank you. Sometimes they do. Course there be plenty a other junk, too . . . candy wrappers, empty water bottles, raggy clothes, dirty syringes . . . and the smells, woo-eee. Let's just say old pee ain't the only human remains left around.

In the shadows I spot a Coke can all torn apart. They pretty typical cookers for meltin' down heroin pellets and makin' 'em liquid. As I move toward it, I more feel than hear the rumblin' of a big rig takin' the exit. I get to the can and kneel down to see if anyone left a cotton— usually a cigarette filter pinched together to absorb the liquid before they suck it into the syringe.

And sure enough, there it is—proof of a loving God, or whatever we're allowed to call him these days.

I uncap my water bottle and slop a little onto the cotton. Then I squish and pinch it to work out any last bit a drug. I pull a clean syringe from my sock and jab in the needle to suck up the cloudy liquid. It won't be much, but 'nough to ease his sickness an hour or two. By then the city would be comin' to life and with it maybe some business.

I work my way back to JJ, and after five or six tries I find a vein not too scarred to take the needle, and I push the junk into his body.

He closes his eyes and takes a breath.

"Better?" I ask.

He nods.

But we both know it ain't enough. I rise and take a few steps down the embankment where I can stand up straight and stretch my back. I see the tenements a hundred yards away and the strip mall beyond.

JJ knows 'xactly what I'm thinkin.'

"I'm sorry, babe," he mumbles.

"Ain't nothin'." I look out over the city. "We get you somethin' by the time that wears off.

"Sorry . . ."

"No sweat, baby. We get you somethin' soon, I promise."

four

B
E
R
N
A
R
D

Great news! The digital board across from Nurse Hardgrove's station said we'd be having a new member joining the family. Better yet, he was going to be my roomie! Pretty exciting since it's been kind of lonely after they moved my old one to Sacramento. That's where they send folks when the therapy and medication here don't help which they usually do. You would have liked him. He was a good guy and perfectly normal except for the prayer tassels he kept weaving from my dental floss, or our soda straw wrappers, or anything else he could get his hands on. Poor fella.

And it's not like we didn't try to help. Dr. Aadil really went out of his way. He always does. In fact he's one of the best doctors we've ever had, and believe me, I should know since I practically grew up here. Well, since I was fourteen. I'm what they call 'chronic.' Anyways, nothing we did here helped. Now, though, he's a lot better. At least that's what they tell us, but it would sure be nice to get a letter from him like he promised before he left.

But about the new guy... Maxwell Portenelli. He's supposed to be some famous fashion designer. A couple of the girls in the pod claimed they knew his name. Maybe they did, maybe they didn't. I'm not saying they're making it up, but to be honest, none of my tube socks have heard of him. Or my boxers. It's true, they may not read the same magazines as the girls (they're more into GQ), but I mean clothes are clothes, right?

Anyways, I didn't get a chance to talk to him until Circle. The daughter, who helped move him in, asked for some privacy so I headed down to the TV room. She was one of those walking skeleton types with real skimpy clothes, giant sunglasses, and more ink on her arms than the Wall Street Journal—and a lot more color, so I guess that would make them more like USA Today or maybe Ralphy's comic books, which he tapes to the back of the toilet tank and passes around to all of us . . . Well, except Darcy, who'd just rip them up or hold them ransom for some of his meds. But I digress.

The point is—and there is a point—we really didn't get to meet each other until afternoon Circle. Of course, everyone was on their best behavior. Chloe had brushed her hair. Joey had brushed his teeth. Ralphy wore his same goggles and shower cap, but he replaced his old cape with a brand new bath towel, something he only did for special occasions. Nelson had polished his shoes a couple more times than usual, Winona had put away her inter-galactic communicator/tampon dispenser, and thanks to his attack on me this morning, Jamal had been put away in Contemplative Lock Up. His girlfriend, Darcy, had waxed her head to a reflective sheen and wore a black, long-sleeved leotard top to accentuate her muscular physique (while at the same time silencing any distracting tattoo chatter).

And me? I did my best not to eavesdrop on the various kitty-cat charms dangling from Winona's bracelet, let alone watch the fire extinguisher across the room that kept waving its nozzle at me in a provocative manner.

The good news was, Max was as crazy as the rest of us. Maybe worse—always smiling and grinning like they had him on way too much Thorazine. And laugh? Man, did he like to laugh. The slightest thing would set him off. It got to the point where I was feeling kind of sorry for Dr. Aadil. Seriously, he couldn't address any of Max's issues without the guy grinning like it was all some kind of joke. Don't get me wrong, Max wasn't being rude or anything. It was just his illness talking.

When he finally got around to telling about the fortune cookie, Dr. Aadil asked as gently as possible, "But why would this great cosmic force you describe speak through something as inconsequential as a fortune cookie?"

Max broke into another one of his grins. "That's exactly what I asked."

"And?"

"He likes surprises. 'Messing with reality,' He calls it."

I tried not to giggle, but I couldn't help myself. Neither could the kitty-cat charms on Winona's bracelet.

Luckily, Dr. Aadil didn't notice. Instead, he asked, "And you know this because . . . ?"

"He told me."

"During your psychic break?"

"No, this morning when I was moving into Bernie's room." He grinned over at me. "By the way He really likes that painting you made. The one with the ocean and the sky."

I sat a little straighter. "He does?"

Winona interrupted, "Certainly you're cognizant of the fact that the entire canvas is painted the same color blue."

He nodded, smiling. "And that's His favorite color."

I glanced away, hoping no one thought I was getting prideful. But out of the corner of my eye I saw the extinguisher flipping me off, so I'm pretty sure I failed.

Meanwhile, Chloe turned to Dr. Aadil and blurted out the answer to a question no one had asked. "Why are you asking me?" We were used to her doing this, but it always made her embarrassed and she slumped into her chair, pulling her hair over her face.

Dr. Aadil turned back to Max. "So, if it spoke to you today are you—"

"He," Max said.

"Pardon me?

"He's a person, not an it."

"I see. In any event, are you saying you still have these episodes? That this 'encounter' you experienced was not a one-time event?"

Max smiled. "It was a one-time event, entering heaven. But now I visit Him whenever I want."

Ralphy adjusted his shower cap. "You visit . . . God?"

Looking up to the ceiling and bobbing his head, Nelson quoted, "All discussion of specific deity and/or deities in a public forum is strictly forbidden—California Health and Safety Code, Section 1179.10."[1]

"Thank you, Nelson," Dr. Aadil said.

He pushed up his glasses. "You're welcome."

"But remember, in these sessions the topic is entirely legal. After all that's why we're here, right? To get well?"

"That is correct. The stated purpose of Circle time is to—"

"Thank you, Nelson."

"You're welcome."

Dr. Aadil turned back to Max. "So tell me, where exactly do you go for these visits?"

Max looked at him a little puzzled. "Where?"

"Yes."

"Well . . . right here."

"Here?"

"He's all around."

"Here."

"Yes, He hides in plain sight."

"He hides."

"Only from those who don't want to see Him."

"And you want to see him."

"Not until I went to Heaven. Now I want to be with Him all the time."

The doctor nodded. "And you say he likes Bernard's painting."

"He loves it."

"Because it's blue."

"Because he loves Bernard. He's His favorite child."

"But . . . didn't you say he said *you* were his favorite child?"

"That's right."

"Then how—"

"When you're infinite, everybody can be your favorite."

We all turned to Dr. Aadil and waited as he wrote something down. When he finished, he nodded to Chloe. "And how does that make you feel, Chloe?"

She looked at him kind of confused, like she'd already given her answer.

He turned back to Max. "You see, Maxwell, Chloe's faith system doesn't believe in a personal deity."

Max smiled. "It doesn't stop Him from loving her."

"But she doesn't believe in him."

"He believes in her."

The doctor paused and wrote something else down. Chloe shifted in her seat and everyone got real quiet, except for the charms on Winona's bracelet, which were making those cute, little mewing sounds.

Oh, and the janitor, outside in the courtyard. He'd been with us less than a week but he always played his recorder during his lunch break. It's not a tape recorder type of recorder. It's one of those Renaissance flute kind of things—which would be a lot better if he knew more than just one song. But he didn't, which always meant he played the same thing, which always sounded kind of breathy and airy. I mean it was pretty and every-thing, and I don't want to be rude, but it's just not the type of song you'd hear on the radio . . . or anywhere else for that matter. Still, practice makes perfect and I'm sure he'd get better. At least I hoped so.

Dr. Aadil finished what he was writing and turned to Ralphy. "So tell me, Raphael, how do you feel about this god?"

"California Health and Safety Code, Section—"

"Thank you, Nelson, but I was speaking to Raphael."

Nelson folded his arms and slumped into a pout.

Ralphy readjusted his bath towel and answered, "Raphael Montoya Hernandez III is sworn to uphold the laws of the land."

"Of course. And if someone breaks those laws, how does that make you feel?"

Ralphy swallowed, gave a nervous look to Max, and repeated. "I am sworn to uphold the laws of the land."

The doctor nodded and turned to me. "And Bernard? How do Maxwell's encounters make you feel?"

I frowned, my mind racing a million miles an hour, until I'd found the perfect answer. "He likes my painting."

"He likes them all." Max smiled. "They're all His favorite."

"Dr. Aadil turned to Darcy and asked, "Darcy?"

She just shook her head and kept staring at Max. We all knew she was sizing him up, trying to decide how best to talk him out of his medication.

"Joseph?"

The little black kid of African American persuasion had spent all Circle clinging to his chair like he was about to fall off.

Dr. Aadil continued. "Do you have any thoughts on this issue?"

"Oh, not really." His voice was high and kind of wavery.

"You seem to be hanging on tightly today."

Joey gave a weak smile. "It's almost Summer Solstice."

"So the planet is really tilting?"

He gripped the chair tighter. "Yes, sir."

Joey was rescued from some group that still believes the earth is flat. Poor kid can't get it out of his head. So when he thinks the earth is tilting, he really thinks it's tilting.

Dr. Aadil turned back to Max. "We all appreciate your thoughts, Maxwell. But you must not forget the centuries of innocent people who have suffered, those who were tortured and killed over religion. Countless wars have been waged in the name of—"

Max started to chuckle and the doctor stopped.

"I'm sorry," Max said. "I don't mean to be discourteous, but no one is talking about religion."

"We're not?"

"Religion has nothing to do with a father and a child. A father and child are family, not religion."

Dr. Aadil started to answer, then paused.

I glanced around the group. Everybody was listening as hard as me.

Finally, the doctor answered, "Even a family has rules."

Max nodded.

The doctor continued, "And there must be punishment when those rules are broken."

Max started to nod again, then stopped and shook his head. "No."

"No?"

"There's discipline . . . not punishment."

"Please, explain to us the difference?"

"Discipline helps the child become better, to grow up into all he or she can be."

"And punishment?"

"Comes from anger."

"And your god is never—"

"All discussion of deity and/or deities—"

Dr. Aadil threw Nelson a look and he stopped.

"I think—" Max paused. "I think it takes a lot for a good parent to become angry. And for a perfect God to become angry . . . it takes even more."

Nelson interrupted, "The Lord is gracious and compassionate, slow to anger and rich in—"[2]

"Nelson."

(If you're guessing State codes weren't the only things he'd memorized, you'd be right).

"Maxwell, you certainly know that other religions have embraced the concept of a personal god. Some of those religions are the very ones that nearly destroyed us."

Max nodded. "I know, and He and I have talked a lot about that."

"You and god?"

"Yes."

"And?"

"He says it's because people only know Him as a concept. They've never bothered to know Him as a person. He says they know *about* Him, but never *experience* Him.

We all turned back to Dr. Aadil who jotted down the information.

"He also says," Max hesitated. "May I?"

Dr. Aadil looked up and nodded. "Certainly."

"He says our biggest problem is we don't see ourselves through His eyes, through the eyes of a loving parent."

"And if we did?"

"If we did, it would make us as enthusiastic about ourselves as He is."

five

A
L
E
X
I
S

Troy Hudson was too much beautiful for one man. It wasn't the vodka or the blow or the club lighting. He was a god. And as Robert brought him to my table I knew I was called to be his high priestess.

When they arrived, Robert pointed his Perrier at me and shouted over the music, "And this is my baby sister, Alexis."

Troy gave me no time to return to my default position of looking bored or at least mildly distracted. Instead, he pushed past the half dozen randoms sitting around me and shook my hand. "Love your work!" he yelled, then smiled and gave me a thumbs up.

I tried not to wince at the cliché.

My efforts went unnoticed. He winked and gave me a knowing nod. "Big fan!"

Okay, so maybe gods aren't so great at making conversation. But between that perfect bone structure and those ridiculous blue eyes, was such a detail really necessary? I nodded and casually shrugged while finishing my drink. I knew better than to return the compliment. Truth be told, I'd not seen a movie of his since I was eighteen, some five or six years ago. And, more truth be told, I was so wasted I wasn't sure I could sound cool or disinterested enough to be hot and interesting.

Fortunately, Robert, whose job was to keep the company afloat until Father got back on his feet, weaseled back into the conversation. "Troy says he can get us Vittoria Haven for the Fall campaign."

It took all my strength to stare blankly. For the uninitiated, Vittoria won a Golden Globe last Spring and her recent film picked up the Palme d'Or at Cannes. She wasn't big in the States. Not yet. But after the Academy Awards she would be huge. There wasn't a fashion designer in the world who wouldn't die, or at least go through rehab, to have her wear their clothes. Does she have the body for it? Not even close. Does it matter? Not with Photoshop. When Father first started back in Milan, designers fought for the top models. Today, it's for the hottest stars and Vittoria was on fire.

To demonstrate my unbridled enthusiasm, I leaned forward to pick up another drink. I'm Alexis Portenelli, daughter of Maxwell Portenelli. I'm freaking fashion royalty. I don't get impressed. Unfortunately, I misjudged the distance of the glass and knocked it over. Pulling back my hand, I knocked over another glass, ice cubes clattering across the table and sliding along with the booze into a few laps.

I laughed and of course all the new hirelings followed my lead. I didn't know their names, but they'd give me the SSX shirts off their emaciated backs. They had to. They were the blessed, the privileged, the chosen. I had an underling hire them out of Parsons and the other NY kennels just last week. With the temporary change in leadership, it was time to clean out the old design team and replace it with the new. I was their future. And though I would never voice it, they were mine.

I rose from the table. So did the hirelings. Those with outfit casualties filed with me toward the bathroom for clean up—pretty girls to the left, pretty boys to the right, trysts take your pick. Not that I minded the excursion. Another visit to the loo was another excuse for another line. The booze was fine, but nothing gave you confidence like good, old-fashioned cocaine. I needed to step up my game with Troy and a little snort was just the boost I needed.

"Alexis." Robert caught my arm just before I entered.

I turned to him. I was the picture of cool and calm, and might have pulled it off if the walls weren't drifting in one direction and the floor another.

"We've got the board meeting at 11:00 tomorrow," he said.

"I just dropped Father off at happy acres. Believe me, I need this."

He nodded but wasn't convinced.

"You don't know what it was like, leaving him there with those psychos. No matter what I say or do, he doesn't even—" my throat tightened but I pushed on. "He still doesn't know who I am." I hate self-pity and looked out to the dance floor—but not before I caught the flicker of pain in Robert's own eyes. He was only Father's stepson, but he loved him like the real deal.

We stood, staring at the dancers.

"You worry too much, big brother."

"That's my job."

"And you're so good at it." I reached out to pat his cheek, but missed, nearly poking his eye out with my acrylics.

Now that Father was on medical leave, the creative reins of the company were in my hands. And since I was the *artiste,* it was agreed Robert would help provide me whatever I needed—including the natural or artificial stimulation necessary to call up my creative muse— particularly with the New York Fashion Show just around the corner. Unfortunately, my creative muse had moved without leaving a forwarding address. With the most important event in our company's history coming up, she wasn't even returning my calls.

"Alexis," one of the hirelings called from inside.

I smiled. "Duty calls." I started to turn then said, "You really think he can get us Vittoria?"

"He's good. He can get whoever he wants."

"Yes, he can." I gave a coquettish smile. "And he will."

"Lex . . ."

"What?"

"Dial it back a little, okay?"

"For you, Robert, the world."

"Alexis!" another hireling called.

"Ugh. Coming!" I turned and entered the bath-room.

The floor to ceiling mirrors and vintage lighting were staples in every respectable club. As always, the stalls were filled to capacity with various extracurricu-lar activities and, of course, post-binge weight manage-ment. Meanwhile, the mirrored counters ensured that no bits of pricey powder were wasted. It annoyed me having to come here and mingle with normies to get my rocks off. But the clubs were infested with smartphone, wanna-be paparazzi, and the Amazonian bathroom attendant was always present to ensure privacy.

After a couple lines, I adjusted some stray hair and re-applied the Anusol under my eyes. (Hemorrhoid cream does wonders for bags; all the models and tran-nies swear by it.) Double-checking my nose, I headed out through the mirrored door.

And there he was, standing just a few yards away. He watched the dance floor with disinterested disdain. I took my cue and just happened to stumble upon him, pretending disinterested disdain in his disinterested disdain.

Yes sir, there was no doubt about it. The night was young and by the look of things, it was going to be very good.

six

B
E
R
N
A
R
D

There was a knock on our door and Biff (or was it Britt?) stuck his head inside. "Lights out in thirty."

I nodded from the painting easel where I stood. "Thank yo—"

He shut the door and continued down the hall.

I glanced across the room to Max. Sometimes, for the new guys, getting checked on every thirty minutes can be nerve-wracking but not for me because I'm the type that always likes to know where I am just in case I get lost.

Max didn't seem to mind either. He was too busy sitting at one of the little white cubicles we call our desk and writing in his notebook. Actually almost everything here at the facility is white. And pretty much cubicle— or at least they have lots of corners, which is probably why I like painting circles so much. Though, I've got to be honest, I really wasn't so thrilled with the ones I was painting tonight. They looked a lot more eggish than circleish. That happens sometimes when Darcy shakes me down for the evening's medication. Then I can't draw a circle for the life of me.

She'd shaken down Max, too. It's like a ritual. She stands around the corner of Nurse Hardgrove's station, hand open, waiting for us to spit out what we've pretended to swallow. What she does with the pills is beyond me. Though Joey's pretty sure he's seen her selling them to the staff. She's quite the businesswoman and she makes lots of money selling lots of stuff. And if anybody ever complains, there's always Jamal who makes sure they only do it once.

But Max didn't seem to mind—giving up his night meds, I mean. He just chuckled, stuffed his hands into his pockets, and strolled down the hall to our room.

Now he was sitting at his desk writing stuff down and doing even more chuckling. He must have come up with something good, because he suddenly broke out into good, old-fashioned laughter.

"What's so funny?" I asked. "What are you writing?"

He wiped his eyes, chuckled a little more, and finally answered, "It's just all the stupid things I did today."

"And that makes you laugh?"

"It makes God laugh."

I cringed, glancing up to the video camera in the corner of the room. They say the guys in Surveillance don't pay a lot of attention, at least to the male patients. But Max was new and you can never tell when they might have the volume up.

I turned from it and lowered my voice. "You hear God laugh?"

He grinned. "All the time."

I just looked at him, kind of tilting my head.

"And not just me. All of heaven hears Him. And when He gets going, well, it's pretty hard not to join in."

I nodded like it was an everyday thing. "Should I try to get your meds back from Darcy?"

He broke into more laughter. When he was done, he said, "You don't believe me?"

"Oh, no," I said, "I mean, well yes, maybe. I mean . . ." I chose my words carefully. Don't get me wrong, he was a great guy and everything, but since this was our first night as roomies, I wanted to make sure I woke up nice and alive in the morning. "It's just I never thought of"—I glanced up to the camera and lowered my voice again—"God laughing. I never thought of Him having those type of feelings."

"*We* have those type of feelings."

"Well, yeah, but—"

"And we were created in His image."

I frowned. "But when I think of God and feelings . . . I just naturally figure He's mad and grumpy."

"Why?"

I shrugged.

"You don't think God is happy?"

"Max." I motioned to the camera.

"When He thinks of you, don't you think that makes Him smile?"

"I don't think He thinks of me."

"Seriously?' Why would you say that?"

It was a pretty silly question and I had a thousand different reasons. But the one that leaped into my mind was the giant photograph outside the National Science Museum we sometimes visit on our field trips. It's this huge picture of the universe with over 1500 galaxies. Some are ginormous, others are just smudgy, pinpoints of light. Nelson said each one had about 100 billion stars. 1500 galaxies times 100 billion stars is . . . well, it's a lot. Anyways, near the bottom, right hand corner of the mural, there's this tiny little dot, and beside it is an arrow pointing with the words:

"YOU ARE HERE"

About a year ago some graffiti artist-type snuck in and painted the word *barely* above it, so now it reads:

barely
"YOU ARE^HERE"

And for whatever reason, nobody has ever changed it.

"Bernie?"

I looked back to Max and he continued, "If you knew how happy you make Him, you'd be laughing, too."

"Me?"

"Of course, you. He's always bragging about you. Do you know he actually goes around humming and singing about you?"

"God," I whispered. "Singing? About . . . me?"

"And sometimes, when He's in the mood, He gets a whole bunch of angels to join Him as backup."

I knew my mouth had dropped open but there wasn't much I could do about it. "Why would," I cleared my throat. "Why would He sing about me?"

"Because He loves you."

"You said that before, but what have I done to be loved?"

He laughed. "Not a thing."

I frowned. "Then why—"

"What does a baby do to be loved by his mother?"

"Nothing. 'Cept maybe poop his diapers and cry a lot."

"Exactly. And why does she love and make such a big deal about him? Why does she bore the rest of us with all her stories and photographs of him?"

"Because . . . he's hers?"

"Bingo."

I blinked, trying to comprehend.

Max smiled. "He told me once—I don't fully understand this—but He told me one time that He loves me more than He loved his own life."

Now my mouth was really open.

"Those were His exact words: 'More than my own life.'"

I glanced down, then over to my painting. Either Max was a lot sicker than I thought or . . . or I didn't know what to think.

"He loves everything you do, Bernie. The way you brush your teeth, the way you tie your shoes—"

"It's supposed to be around and through, but I go through and around."

"—the way you talk to Darcy's tattoos—"

"He told you that?"

"This afternoon."

"But that's nuts. Everybody knows I have an imbalance of neurotransmitters that—"

"Maybe. But it can also be a gift."

"A gift?"

"Do you think you were just an accident? Do you think He was sleeping on the job when you were wired that way?"

"I don't, I didn't—"

"If you let Him teach you how to use it, I promise you someday it will actually become a gift."

"Really?"

"And when that happens . . . watch out."

"But . . . if I don't learn . . . I mean?"

"He'll still love you." Max nodded to my easel. "What are you painting there?"

"They're supposed to be circles."

"Ah, of course. But maybe they're more. Did you ever think of that?"

I looked at them, then to him, then blinked again.

"You'll see," he said.

"But . . . they're just circles."

"Bernie, they're coming from your mind, from the imagination He gave you. And He says that's a very holy place."

"A holy . . ." I stopped then continued, "My mind?" I looked down. "Sometimes my mind doesn't think such holy stuff."

"Mine neither. That's what this list is all about."

I looked back to it. "The silly things?"

"I didn't say they were silly. I said they were stupid. And yes, sometimes thinking them or doing them makes Him sad. They make me sad."

We were interrupted by another knock on the door.

He smiled and got to his feet. "But not for long."

I watched as he crossed the room and opened the door. There stood our little janitor, the trash man, come to pick up our garbage. He was a short, smiley, Mexican guy in white overalls. Behind him was his cart with toilet paper, soap, paper towels, and a big plastic bag for collecting our trash.

Max grinned, "And here he is." He opened the door wider for him to come in.

The trash man looked to me for permission. I nodded and he entered, pushing his cart, which had one obnoxious squeaky wheel. When he spotted my painting he broke into another smile.

"You like?" Max said.

"Sí." He grinned. "Qué rico!"

"It really is, isn't it?" Max said.

"Sí, Sí."

I looked at my painting. I wasn't exactly sure what they saw, but I felt a lot better about them seeing it.

"So," Max said, "have you two officially met?"

The trash man looked at me and smiled.

"Not officially," I said. "But I hear him playing in the courtyard at lunch."

His smile broke into another grin. "Bueno, no?"

I nodded and lied, just a little. "Bueno."

He beamed back at me, all happy and proud.

"So . . ." Max headed back to his desk. "Are we ready?"

The man nodded. "Sí."

"All right then." Max reached down and ripped off a sheet from the notebook he'd been writing in. He wadded it up and tossed it into the trash bag. "And there we go."

Trashman grinned. So did Max. They seemed to be doing a lot of that.

"I'm sorry," I said. "What just happened?"

"All my mistakes. Didn't you see? I just threw them away. Now our friend here is going to take them, burn them in the incinerator, and it'll be like they never happened."

"But . . . they did happen."

"Not if he burns them."

I looked over to Max's notebook, than to the garbage bag, then back to the notebook.

"You want to give it a shot?" Max asked.

"I'm sorry?"

"Do you want to burn your mistakes, too?"

"I . . . I could do that?"

"Sure. Why not?" He looked to Trashman. "If it's okay with you?"

The little guy nodded and broke into another one of his grins.

It was a crazy idea, even *I* knew that. But if a person's going to do crazy, this is the place. And since it was

Max's first night and since I didn't want him to feel like he was being weird or anything . . .

"Here." He pulled out his chair and offered me a seat.

I looked at him, then to Trashman who nodded. Figuring I had nothing to lose, I sat down and picked up the pencil. "So I just, uh . . ."

"Write down any stupid thing you remember doing today."

I stared hard at the paper.

"It's not that difficult, really. Just anything you wish you hadn't done."

"Well . . ." I took a deep breath. "In the lunch line, when Winona wasn't looking, I stole a second banana pudding."

"Great," Max said. "Write it down."

I gripped the pencil and wrote: "Stealing dessert."

"Good job," Max said.

Trashman nodded.

"Anything else?"

"Well . . . in the TV room, when she wasn't looking . . ."

"Go on."

"I'm not a perv or anything, but, well I kinda stared a little too long at, you know, Chloe."

Max nodded. "Excellent."

"Sí," Trashman agreed. "Sí, Sí."

I took another breath and wrote it down. I don't know . . . maybe it was because the guys were smiling and not making fun of me, but I actually felt a little better. Then I thought of another. "And later, when Britt or Biff told me I was going to be late for Circle, I made a face at him behind his back."

Trashman nodded and Max clapped, "Perfect. Now you're getting it."

I wrote it down and giggled a little. Not because I was proud of it or anything, but because it felt good to tell somebody . . . you know, to get it off my chest. Other things came to mind and I wrote them down, too. Sometimes I felt stupid and embarrassed, but writing them down and Max saying stuff like, "Oh, yeah," or, "I've been there," really helped.

It wasn't until Biff (or was it Britt?) opened the door and said he might have to write us up for breaking curfew, that I finally stopped. Of course we apologized and I hoped it did some good since Britt or Biff can really be a stickler for the rules. Anyways, when he left I quickly wadded up my paper and tossed it into the bag.

Trashman beamed and Max slapped me on the back. We took a few seconds saying goodbye before Trashman wheeled his squeaking cart out and Max promised to see him again tomorrow.

Later, as I brushed my teeth and changed into my pajamas, I felt as good as I did with any med. Well, almost. I knew I'd broken curfew and the little pirate nightlight in our bathroom gave me a stern lecture about following the rules and, of course, he was right, and I felt bad. But even then I was thinking I could write it down on tomorrow's list.

seven

B
E
R
N
A
R
D

I could have stayed forever lost in the forest of those giant fir trees. Even though I saw my breath, I felt safe and warm and cozy. And the fog. There was so much of it that the trees quickly turned gray, then blurred, then disappeared all together. I couldn't hear any sounds, not even birds—just absolute stillness and, of course, my own breathing. It was a wonderful place. More real than anything I'd ever seen when I was awake and at the same time it seemed more magical, too.

Then I heard music. The weird, breathy song of Trashman playing his old-fashioned instrument. And clapping. Someone was clapping to it. I squinted hard into the grayness and just barely made out the dark, hazy shape of a hill. I started toward it. The twigs and branches snapped under my feet, and the undergrowth kept tugging at my ankles like it wanted me to stay. But I kept walking as it got lighter and lighter until I finally ran out of trees and stood at the edge of the forest. There was no fog here, just the music and clapping and brightly lit hill. It made me nervous, all that sunlight and openness, but after I took a deep breath for courage, I stepped out of the covering and into the light.

The hill was grassy and so green it almost glowed. And up on top, silhouetted against a blue sky, Trashman sat cross-legged playing his recorder. Max was there, too. He was clapping and dancing all around. It wasn't great dancing, because, let's face it, Max is pretty old, but to be polite, I'll call it dancing.

"Max!" I shouted. "Hey, Max!"

They both looked down and saw me. Max waved. "Come on up," he shouted. "It's beautiful up here."

I looked back to the forest, which still was nice and cozy with the fog and everything.

"Come on, Bernie!"

I turned back to Max who kept waving and calling to me.

Since it was a dream and I had nothing to lose I shouted, "Okay."

He nodded and went back to his clapping and dancing as Trashman kept on playing.

The hill really wasn't too big, eighty, maybe a hundred feet, but it was pretty steep. I'd only taken a few steps when I heard shouting behind me, "Come back . . . don't leave us . . . come back."

I turned around, but of course nobody was there. Just the trees. But anybody who's seen those old *Wizard of Oz* or *Lord of the Rings* movies knows trees can be just as chatty as people.

"Don't leave us," they shouted. "It's safe in here. Come back."

They were probably right, but Max and Trashman were having such a good time and, like I said, it was only a dream, so I called back, "I'm sorry, but I really gotta go."

"But it's safe."

"I know, but—"

"It's so safe . . ."

If there's one thing I've learned about inanimate objects, they never let up until you ignore them. So that's what I did. Of course, they still kept shouting, but eventually, they got bored and settled down.

The climb really wasn't too hard, but I still had to stop every once in a while to catch my breath. That's when I'd stand and just watch and listen to the two of them. They really were having a great time. It wasn't until I was about half way up that I heard kind of a booming rumble. The ground started shaking and that's about the time I knew we were having an earthquake. Not a big deal. Not when you've grown up in California and survived The Big One of '32. But still . . .

"Guys!" I shouted. "Hey, Guys!"

But they were too busy playing and dancing to notice or even care. I wouldn't have cared either except for the boulders. Some of them had shaken lose and started bouncing down the hill. Again, not a big deal, except they were bouncing straight toward me!

"Guys!"

They just kept playing and dancing. I turned back to my tree buddies in the forest, but they weren't so helpful, either—unless you call their snorting in disgust and yelling, "We told you so, we told you so," helpful.

I spotted a tiny gully to my right. It was only three or four feet deep and no wider than my body, but it would have to do. I leaped into it, burying my head under my arms, hoping the rocks would somehow miss and bounce past me.

They missed all right, but they didn't exactly bounce past. Instead, they piled up over me . . . first one, then another and another—pretty hefty fellows that blotted out the sky in no time. They didn't actually touch me, but they were doing a pretty good imitation of burying me. Of course, I did my part, yelling and screaming, until the dust and dirt got me coughing so bad I had to stop.

After what seemed like forever, everything finally came to an end, except for my coughing. That's when the boulder just above my head started to talk. Unfortunately, he didn't seem too interested in helping.

Instead of a polite, "How do you do?" he greeted me with, "As soon as I wiggle loose, I'm gonna fall and crush your skull."

The one beside him, over my back, wasn't much friendlier. "So tell me crazy boy, you like your new accommodations?"

"Max!" I shouted and coughed some more. "Max, can you hear me?"

"Maybe he don't like the decorating," the first boulder said.

"That it, crazy boy? You don't like Early American Crypt?"

"Max!"

"Bernie?" Max's voice was faint but clear. "Bernie, can you hear me?"

"I'm down here! I'm trapped!"

A third boulder, just above my hips chuckled, "You got that right, pal."

"I can't get out!"

"Pretty bright for a mental," another said.

"Yes you can!" Max shouted. "You can get out!"

"No!" I shook my head, which was kind of silly since he couldn't see me. Also since it made a bunch more dirt and gravel trickle down around me. "They're too heavy!" I coughed some more. "They're too big!"

That's right," another one over my legs sneered.

"We been working out," the second one bragged.

"It's not true!" Max yelled. "They just look heavy."

"What?"

"It's a disguise. They want you to think you can't move them so you won't try. But you can. I promise you can move them."

I shouted, "Not by myself. You gotta help me."

"That defeats His purpose."

"What? Whose purpose?"

"Give it a shot, Bernie. Try to move them."

"But—"

"Trust me."

It was a silly idea. He had no clue how big they were. But silly or not, it didn't look like I had a lot of choices. So I twisted and turned in the dirt until I was on my back facing up at the boulders. I reached toward the one above my head.

"Touch me and they'll send you to Sacramento," the boulder said.

"What?"

"I'll have that doctor ship you out so fast your scrambled brains will spin."

I hesitated. Was it true? Did he have that type of power? I decided not to take the chance and reached for the boulder above my chest.

"Touch me and I'll have Jamal give you free dental work."

"Max!"

"Don't listen to them!" he shouted. "They're all bluff. They can't do a thing to you."

"Why won't you help me?"

"I am," Max said. "Listen to the music."

"Yeah, right." The boulder above my legs cackled. "Trashman can't play worth beans."

Another snickered, "Is that refried, black, or pinto?" Which made the others break out laughing and slapping their knees or whatever rocks slap.

And me? I just sort of lay there hoping Max or somebody would come and get me out . . . until, finally, I woke up.

eight

S
A
F
F
R
O
N

"What he go and do that for?" JJ says as he's climbin'
out of the dumpster.

"I don't know, baby."

"Pourin' Clorox all over it. That were some pretty
good food in there, too."

"I know."

Mariposa weighs in. As part-time nanny and full-
time camp guest, he's always willin' to help out . . . long
as he don't dirty them hands (he's a major germaphobe),

or break a nail. "There is absolutely no excuse for such behavior." He straightens his blouse checkin' for stains. "Except that the man is a sorry sack of human excrement."

JJ gave his hands a sniff then did his best to wipe off the bleach smell. "Like he don't understand the circle of life."

I call back into the dumpster, "Brandylin, honey, nothin' in there. Get out and let's go to the hospital."

I still hear her pushin' stuff around. "Momma, I'm hungry."

"We find somethin' good up there. C'mon."

I see her poke that gorgeous face of hers up over the edge. The early mornin' sun makes her ebony skin glow like one of them cover girls, and it puts a knot in my gut. I know a mother s'pposed to be proud, specially if her baby is knockout pretty, but down here in the Tenderloin it scares me. 'Cause no matter how I try to protect her, someday she gonna pay for it. I already got her on birth control. "To smooth you out," I says. But we both know the real truth.

She starts climbin' outta the dumpster and complains, "There ain't no food up at the hospital."

"They got all sorts a bed pans and medical junk we can recycle."

"If we get there 'fore the others," JJ says, as he and Mariposa reach up and help her down.

"Then maybe after we all go and get us a McD's," I say.

"With fries?" she says.

"Maybe."

"And a shake?"

"We'll see."

"We gotta have a shake. Ain't worth it without a shake."

Not only is my baby pretty, she's a good hustler, too.

So with Mariposa's and JJ's shoppin' carts rattlin' behind us, we head up the hill on the narrow street to Mercy General—one big, happy family. JJ's feelin' pretty good now that he got his medicine, and I turned enough last night and the day 'fore to keep him goin' a while.

But that's the end he says. "No more manhandlin' for you." And I agree. Like all the other times, I agree.

We reach the hilltop at the back of the hospital. Nice thing 'bout dumpster divin', it's honest work. You won't ever see us panhandlin' or postin' no sign on the streets. Not that we don't occasionally boost essentials or hit a lick, but only when the circumstances call for it. Mostly, it's findin' stuff like appliances and things we

can sell on the corner. Or recycle. We're what the soci-
ologists call, yer modern day hunters and gatherers.

"Hey, beauty! Black beauty!"

We turn an' see some white trash van livers drive
by. Course they ain't shoutin' to me or to Mariposa
(much to his disappointment) but to Brandylin. Pretty
disgustin', hangin' out the windows like dogs in heat
and right there in front of her momma. Course me and
JJ, we yell somethin' equally disgustin', which I won't tell
you 'cause like I promised earlier 'bout the language,
and they just drive off cacklin' like crows.

Brandylin, she look pretty disgusted, too . . . but
also a little proud. Like I say, I worry 'bout her.

A few minutes later me and JJ are in the hospital
dumpsters. I tell Mariposa, who is like twice JJ's size,
to keep watch over my girl. 'Course Brandylin wants to
help, but I got my standards. No way she gonna come
down with the hep or somethin' equally ugly. Not at her
age. It's pretty nasty inside, but after some diggin' I find
some beat-up I.V. stands and part of a bed. Both got
some weight, which'll make good recyclin'.

But then I hear Mariposa say, "Uh-oh," and the
rumble of a garbage truck roundin' the corner and startin' up our hill. "Better hurry."

"How you doin' babe?" JJ calls to me.

"Got a few things. You?"

"Jus' paper an' plastic. Look like somebody empty a whole drawer of dentures. Wait a minute. Lord have mercy."

"What?"

He says nothin'.

"JJ?"

"Looks like we gonna have a house guest."

"A what?"

I hear Brandylin squeal and Mariposa break out laughin'.

"What's goin' on?"

"The dude sure got a weight problem," JJ shouts.

Brandylin giggles. "Big time anorexia."

I finally stick my head out and see he's got a real, live skeleton. "That's gross!" I shout. "Put it back. JJ, put it back!"

JJ turns the skull toward me and shakes it back and forth like some ventriloquist dummy sayin' no.

Brandylin and Mariposa laugh some more.

"Don't touch it!" I shout.

"It just plastic." JJ turns to the skull. "Ain't that right, fella?" He nods the head like it's answerin'.

"It's from a hospital," I say. "People die in hospitals!"

"Not this one?" He lifts it out of the dumpster and I see it's attached to a metal stand. "Bet these bones say 'Made in China' somewhere. Mari, give me a hand."

Mariposa steps back. "I most certainly will not."

"C'mon, I worked EMS. I know the difference between real and plastic. "Brandy?"

"Brandylin!" I warn.

But she's already reachin' up and pullin' it out. "He's right, momma." She scrapes it over the edge of the dumpster and drops it onto the pavement. "It ain't real."

JJ gives another laugh as he hauls himself out to join 'em. Everybody's laughin' but me.

"Truck almost here," JJ says. "Better hurry, babe."

I toss my stuff out, hopin' to hit him jus' a little, and they load it into their carts. I barely climb out when a black-and-white comes 'round the corner and spots us. We scramble behind the dumpster, but of course they see us and our carts, so they give their siren a little squawk.

Normally we would a stood around and got cited, but with JJ's priors and me havin' to explain that we're homeschoolin' Brandylin (to insure she get a decent education), we look for other options. And with the garbage truck blockin' most of the narrow street below us, we got it.

"Let's go!" JJ yells.

He and Mariposa push off with one cart, me and Brandylin with the other. But after a few steps it becomes obvious our shoppin' cart is rollin' a lot faster than we're pushing, so I shout to Brandylin, "Get in!"

She climbs up and jumps in. I give an extra little push and hop on the back and 'way we go. JJ and Mariposa must a figured the same thing, 'cause I look over my shoulder and see JJ climin' in and them yellin' and carryin' on like little kids. Brandylin, too. She got her arms up like we on some roller coaster ride. Course the cops hit their siren, but it does no good as we shoot past the dump truck, squeezin' between it and a buildin' and leavin' the boys in blue stuck on the other side.

Faster and faster we go, shakin' and bouncin' and hittin' so many potholes I'm afraid of rattlin' my last few teeth outta my head.

"Say, babe?" JJ shouts behind me.

"Yeah?" I shout back.

"How we gonna stop these things?"

It's a pretty good question but I don't have to worry 'cause we comin' up fast on a vacant lot at the bottom of the hill.

"Hang on!" Brandylin shouts.

It seems a good idea. 'Specially when we hit the curb and the whole cart spills, flippin' end over end, along with both of us. I see JJ and Mariposa crashin' and flippin', too.

Finally we come to a stop. After some colorful language and a lot of laughin', I yell, "Everyone okay?"

Brandylin nods. JJ and Mariposa say they good, too.

"'Cept for our new friend," JJ says.

I turn and see him and Mariposa surrounded by the broken skeleton. Somehow, Mariposa got his leg stuck inside its rib cage.

JJ's studyin' the end of a broken bone. "Now, that's odd," he says.

"What?" I say.

"If this is plastic, why's there real bone marrow inside?"

"Real what?" Mariposa says.

JJ keeps starin'. "Looks like I was wrong. This the real thing."

"What?" Mariposa stares down at the ribs wrapped 'round his leg.

"Must be a dead dude after all."

Me and Brandylin give a shudder but not Mariposa. He screams and begins fightin' his way out of the ribs, which don't seem too anxious to let go.

Pretty soon we all laughin' again, 'cept Mariposa who is kickin' and screamin' and goin' into general hysterics, which, I'm sorry, jus' makes us laugh all the harder.

nine

**B
E
R
N
A
R
D**

"Hey there, handsome."

I glanced down at the cards. At first I thought Blue Reverse was talking to me. But the way she kept sneaking over to Green Skip in the center of my hand when I wasn't looking made it pretty clear she had someone else in mind.

"Please," I whispered, pulling her out of the center and putting her back with the other blue cards on the right.

But she definitely thought Green Skip was hot. I barely glanced to the card Nelson had played, before I looked back and spotted her batting her eyes and giving him a full-on flirt.

"Really?" I whispered. "Why don't you guys get a room?"

She giggled. "Sounds good to me."

It was ten thirty in the morning and we were down in the TV room playing a pretty good game of Uno. Of course Nelson had won most of the hands. (Can you win counting cards in Uno?) Joey, Winona and Max had won a couple. Darcy, Ralphy and Chloe each won one. And me? I could've done a lot better if I didn't have to keep my eyes on Blue Reverse and Green Skip. With fourteen cards in my hand I didn't need any of them running off and procreating more. Also, I was keeping an eye on Biff and Britt (or was it Britt and Biff?) The last thing Max needed was to get busted for all his God talk, which was all he was talking about because that's all everybody wanted him to talk about.

Well, everybody but Nelson.

"According to hospital regulations, which, in turn, must adhere to all state and local—"

"Thanks Nelson," Joey said. "We're good." As usual, the little guy was hanging on to his chair for all he was worth. On good days, when things are only slightly tilted, Joey is afraid he'll slide onto the floor. On bad days, he could fall onto the ceiling.

Ralphy was also keeping lookout, which explains why he leaped to his feet and did another quick three-sixty around the table. "Fear not, Raphael Montoya Hernandez III is here to protect and defend."

"Listen up, Raphael Montoya Hernandez," Darcy snarled. "You run around this table one more—"

"Raphael Montoya Hernandez, *THE III*," he corrected.

"You run around this table one more time to look at my cards and—"

"Yellow!" Chloe sweetly called.

I turned to her. "What's that?"

She pointed to her Wild Card. "I'm changing the color to yellow."

I smiled and said as gently as possible, "It's not your turn."

She looked to me, than to Max who quietly nodded. Embarrassed, she scooted down in her chair like she always does when she wants to disappear.

"My dearest, Señora,"—Ralphy adjusted his goggles while speaking to Darcy—"it is impossible for superheroes to cheat."

"I bet they can die," she said.

Because of her leanings toward homicide, Ralphy flipped his towel to the side and took his seat. Meanwhile, Joey let go of his chair just long enough to play a Blue 5. When he finished he turned back to Max and lowered his voice. "You keep talking about this God wanting to love us."

"According to California State—"

"Nelson, shut your pie hole."

Nelson looked at Darcy, then shut his pie hole.

Joey repeated. "You keep talking about this loving God. But what if we're not good enough to be loved?"

Max played a Blue 3 then looked around the table. "When we think back to our own fathers, did we have to earn their love by being good?"

No one answered. Instead, we all kind of stared at the cards in our hands.

Max cleared his throat. "Right. Let me try that again. If we had *PERFECT* fathers would we have to earn their love by always being good?"

Still no takers.

Finally he turned to Darcy. "You have children, don't you?"

"Somewhere. A couple."

"So do your children have to be perfect for you to love them?"

She shifted, running her hand over her bald head, then she looked right at him. "What about you and your kids?"

You could see the pain flicker across his face until he had to look down. "I, uh . . . can't remember."

"You can't remember how you treated your own kids?" Joey said.

"I can't remember who they are."

Things got quiet, so I quickly chimed in. "You got a daughter, Max. I saw her. She's nice. Well, I didn't get to talk to her or anything, but, you know, I'm sure she is. Nice, I mean."

Max looked up and smiled. "Thanks, Bernie."

I smiled back, grateful I could help.

Finally, Darcy answered him. "I love my brats. No matter what they do." She slapped down a Blue 8. "And believe me, they've done a lot."

I looked back at my hand. And a good thing, too. Blue Reverse was giving Green Skip a shoulder shimmy, which was getting him all worked up. I figured enough was enough. I'd been as polite as I could and I'd sure given her enough warnings, so I pulled the card from my hand—

"No, no," she cried, "I'll be good. I'll be—"

—and dropped her on the pile.

Meanwhile, Joey had turned back to Max. "I don't get your point."

Chloe blurted, "Who's big enough to be God's enemy?" We looked at her and she pulled her bangs back over her eyes mumbling, "Sorry."

"My point is"—Max cleared his throat—"even if we're *NOT* good enough, wouldn't a perfect father love us anyway? And instead of abandoning us or punishing us, wouldn't he stick by our side to help us become better?"

"If that is our wish, of course," Ralphy said.

Max continued, "Instead of blaming us, wouldn't he try to help us?"

Joey agreed. "Or fix us."

Nelson bobbed his head, looking up to the ceiling. "God does not see what is wrong with a person, only what is missing."[3]

We all turned to him.

"That's good," I said.

He pushed up his glasses. "Thank you."

Winona adjusted the aluminum foil around her arms. "So you are stating that the Supreme Being is not concerned about placing blame upon us, but rather in upgrading us?"

"That would put him on our side," Ralphy said.

Max nodded. "And we'd be on his."

"Working together." I grinned. "One, big, happy family."

"But," Ralphy said, "why would this perfect father love us in the first place?"

Winona said, "Perhaps he has no taste in carbon based life forms."

Max smiled. "Perhaps. Or perhaps that's just what loving parents do."

"It's true, I can't help myself." Darcy gave a grudging scowl. "It's like I got no choice but to love my kids. That's why I had 'em in the first place."

Max nodded. "And that's why God made us."

"To love?" Joey asked.

"Yes, to love."

Everybody got real quiet again.

"But, Señor Max," Ralphy broke the silence. "Who exactly are these children of His?"

Joey glanced around the room, "If He's God, who isn't?"

"What about His enemies?" Winona played her card, changing the pile from Blue 7 to Red 7.

I looked to Chloe and grinned. "It's like Chloe said, 'Who's big enough to be His enemy?'"

She looked up at me and smiled. I love it when she does that.

"Surely He would have some enemies," Winona said.

"I wonder," Max said. "If He's everyone's father, wouldn't what Darcy said be true? Wouldn't He love all his children?"

"Even if they hate Him?" Joey asked.

Max nodded again. "Isn't that what a perfect father would do?"

Winona said, "At least until the life form screws up."

"You ain't listening, freak." Darcy said. "I love my kids even when they screw up. I just keep hoping they won't."

"So you do what?" Joey asked. "Just keep loving them, so they can just keep screwing up?"

Darcy shook her head. "No. I love 'em, hoping some day they'll get their act together."

Nelson quoted, "The goodness of God leadeth thee to repentance.'" [4]

"Uno!" Chloe shouted.

I looked over to her hand and whispered, "You've got two cards, you need to have one."

She stared at her hand and frowned.

"So . . ." Max kept thinking. "Instead of us being His enemy, aren't we more like POWs."

"Prisoners of war?" Joey said.

"What war, Señor?

"The one inside our heads. The one that keeps telling us we're too bad to be loved as His children."

Darcy played her card. "The one that keeps accusing me of being a loser."

"The devil," Ralphy said.

Nelson fired off another quote. "'For the accuser of our brethren is cast down.'"[5]

"'The accuser of our brethren.'" Max repeated. "And who does he accuse us to?"

I gave the obvious answer. "God."

He frowned. "Maybe. But I don't think a loving father would believe him."

"Some stranger tells me my kids are garbage, I'd throw his butt out on the street," Darcy said, "even if he was right."

"So . . ." Ralphy said, "if this accuser, if he does not succeed in accusing us to God, then who does he accuse us to?"

Darcy answered, "The only ones stupid enough to believe him. You. Me."

That definitely got everyone thinking. I stole a look over to Darcy's tattoos, then Winona's bracelet. Even they were quiet.

"But what about our screwups?" Joey asked, suddenly grabbing the cards on the table so they wouldn't slip off.

"What about them?" Max said.

"We just can't pretend they didn't happen."

"He's right," Winona said. "If there is a malfunction, how is it reset and repaired?"

Max didn't answer. Instead he looked over to me, like I knew. It took a moment, but then I got it, and I grinned to him. He grinned back, motioning that I could answer, which I did. "If you come to our room tonight, we'll show you."

"Show us what?" Joey asked.

Max just smiled. "It's better if you come and see."

Chloe played her card.

"And bring a pencil and some paper," I said. I glanced over to Chloe who was down to her last card. "You can say *UNO* now," I whispered.

She scowled at me.

"What's wrong?"

She whispered back, "I already did."

ten

A
L
E
X
I
S

"Eleven employees? Without warning?" Uncle Al got his pruney, anal-retentive face to light up nice and red as he continued the lecture. "Devoted workers, some who've been with your father since he started the company? Letting them go without prior notice and not a penny of severance pay? Alexis, this is just, just (insert sputtering here) unprecedented."

Of course it was all performance. I'd seen him do it a dozen times with Father. The pudgy diva knew how to put on a good show when he had to. And this morning he was going for a standing ovation.

"It's a lawsuit waiting to happen," another suit agreed.

A third droid weighed in. "And certainly not the tone your father set for the company."

I scooped a spoonful of salmon pâté from the baggie in my purse and fed it to Toulouse who sat on my lap. The Teacup Maltese gobbled it down. At least I had one friend in the room. Of course this infuriated my uncle, which, of course, was my intent.

His face turned an impressive shade of crimson. "Alexis!"

I winced and pulled down my sunglasses. "There's no need to shout."

"No one is shouting!" he shouted. "We're simply looking for some rational explanation of your behavior." He'd gotten his right eye to twitch like it was something he couldn't control. I told you, he's good.

Another minion spoke up. "With the New York show approaching, it seems inconceivable that you would decide to let go your creative staff when—"

"That's exactly *WHY* she made the decision." Robert sat at my immediate left. "I am in the studio with her every day. I see the love and respect this new crew has for her." An obvious lie, but why should Uncle Al be the only one to dish out the BS? "It was a brilliant decision. Genius. One that Father would have made if he were in her position."

"But he did not make it," the droid said.

"Gentlemen." My brother's voice grew quiet and laser-focused. If anyone could speak boardroomese, Robert could. "There's a new world out there. We all know it. We've seen sales slipping the past two, two and a half years. And who here did not take it personally when we had to close down the London flagship and then the Paris shop?"

The brood grew quiet. Some stared hard at the long, polished table before them. It's true, losing the European boutiques was like losing members of the family. But Father had given his solemn word we'd get them back and we all believed him . . . until his meltdown.

Robert continued. "Our father was a great leader, there's no doubt about it. We miss him terribly. Everyone in this room is grateful for his seeing our potential and encouraging us to outperform even our own expectations."

No one looked up.

"And that is the same potential he has seen and expectation that he insists upon for Alexis. That's why she is in charge. You may not see what he saw, but I tell you this: she's exactly what we need. For this time, for this season, she's precisely what we need. Her debut collection will turn the fashion world on its head, easily putting us back on top. And this new team she's assembled knows *PRECISELY* how to deliver her vision."

Bull's eye. My white knight came through again. For those without a program, his mother married my father when Robert was nine and I was five. We were the perfect blended family, well except for the part of his mom dying two months later. Talk about the honeymoon being over. Still, the three of us adjusted and got along fine. Well, the two of us. Father's business and his employees had always been his real family. Not that he didn't try to be a good parent. But as the poster child for Workaholics Anonymous, even when he appeared for the obligatory birthday party or turkey carving, he wasn't there. Work was his life. It consumed him. So did his employees. For that they loved him. And for that I . . . well, I barely knew him. Truth be told, Robert and I were connected more to the shop seamstresses than we ever were to our father.

Fashion was his life. And it became ours. By sixteen I was already designing accessories—necklaces, bracelets, that sort of thing. Robert tried, but didn't quite have the knack. And because I was the owner's kid, I suppose I got extra breaks that pushed and/or forced me up the ladder. Robert understood and despite the occasional spats of jealousy, when the chips were down, he was always at my side—the one I turned to first for inspiration—my confidant, my best and most trusted friend.

Toulouse whimpered. I reached back into my bag and gave him another spoonful of pâté. I'm sure the smell of fish filled the boardroom, but I didn't notice since my nose was pretty much in malfunction these days—another reason to drop the party scene.

That and the blackouts.

Not only did I not know what time I got home this morning, I wasn't sure how I got there. All I knew was I did *NOT* wake up beside Troy Hudson. When Robert showed up to drag my sorry butt out of bed and help me into the shower, I croaked, "What happened to Troy? Was it something I said?"

"No." He carefully propped me against the bathroom wall and reached in to turn on the water.

"I didn't puke on him or anything?"

"No, you were quite enchanting. He even insisted on taking you home."

I started sliding to the right until he caught me and straightened me up.

"But he didn't stay."

"Not for your lack of trying, I'm sure."

Once I was stable, he turned his back so I could undress. I groaned and peeled off my T-shirt. At least I tried. "Why not? Oh please, don't tell me he's gay."

"Doubtful. He was practically drooling. But before driving you home, he made a point to promise me he would not take advantage of you."

"Not take advantage?" The shirt was putting up a good fight. "Kind of the point for getting wasted isn't it?"

"He seems very old school."

The T-shirt sleeves had shifted to impossible places. "But he was into me, right?"

"Most definitely."

I gave up on the shirt. Keeping my eyes closed against the ruthless light and pounding in my head, I felt my way along the tiled wall into the water. "So why didn't he stay?"

"I'm sure he wanted to, but not when you were in that condition."

I leaned my forehead against the cool tile. "That's so weird."

"I think it's called respect."

Back in the boardroom, the opera continued, the star belting out the same aria he'd sung the last several performances. "I received another call from St. Cheron. They offer their condolences."

"I'm sure they do," a suit murmured.

"Vultures," the droid agreed.

"They wished to stress that even though Maxwell's illness has removed him from the picture—"

"Temporarily removed," another corrected.

"*Temporarily* removed him from the picture. They wished to stress that their latest offer still remains." He continued without missing a beat. "And, as I have previously stated—"

"More than once," Robert said.

"As I have previously stated, I believe it is an offer we should not discount too hastily."

We all knew the next verse by heart. Having already drained my water glass, I reached for Robert's.

"They asked me to remind you that an acquisition in no manner means losing creative control. Portenelli Fashions will remain at the cutting edge of the industry, maintaining our unique and original vision." He turned to me. "It would simply bring in resources to free us up, allowing you to commit all of your energies to new and inventive creations, while forcing St. Cheron to carry the fiscal burden of—"

"That's a lie and you know it." The words came before I could stop them—though they might have had more impact if I hadn't winced at their volume. "They'll give us freedom? Right. Maybe for a few months . . . a year." My head throbbed with every syllable, but I pushed on. "We all know the story after that. Our originality becomes their dead weight. Creativity, a dirty word. In two years' time they'll have us catering to Walmart."

"Which isn't necessarily a bad idea," the droid said.

"It is if it destroys this company!" The outburst nearly blew out my eyeballs. I grabbed another gulp of water, which gave Uncle Al time to regroup and become Mr. Sensitive—one of his least accomplished roles.

"Alexis, stop to consider what your father would want. At this juncture in his life, wouldn't he prefer—"

"My father has said no to them for months." I saw Robert wanting to step in, but when I got like this, he knew it was best to stay out of the way. "It would break his heart to sell this company. We all know that." I pushed aside the rising sentimentality and tried to stay focused on the anger. "He spent his whole life building it. Since he was a kid. His *WHOLE LIFE*. He would never sell it. Never. And every one of you know that."

Uncle Al countered, all compassion and reason. "Maybe his little episode says it's time to get some rest. Maybe it's time he starts enjoying the fruits of his labor. Now that things have changed, maybe—"

"What change? The fact that he's not here? That you are?" I was shouting again. "Do you honestly think you can railroad the rest of us into going against his wishes?"

"No one's going against his—"

"That's exactly what you're doing!" It was time for a dramatic exit—which meant not only having to find my feet, but to actually use them. "Our approach may have shifted slightly, but we're still a company. A great company. And when Father comes back, when he's rested and himself, he's going to make us stronger than ever."

Hoping I'd pumped enough adrenalin into my system to pull it off, I pushed back my chair and rose. So far so good. "Mark my words, after the New York show, within a year, we'll be the ones making St. Cheron the offer. *WE* will. Not them. Us! Portenelli Fashions will be king!"

With Toulouse in one arm, I bent down and grabbed my bag with the other . . . a tactical blunder to which my balance immediately reacted. Luckily, Robert appeared, offering physical as well as navigational support. We turned and, together, stormed out of the conference room.

"Do you think they bought it?" I whispered as we stepped into the glass-enclosed hallway.

"Not in the slightest. But I did."

"Me, too. He worked too hard for us to sell it behind his back."

Robert nodded. "You did well. And you didn't fall over, that's always a good sign."

I agreed. "A marked improvement."

eleven

D
R

A
A
D
I
L

Over the past several days, Maxwell Portenelli had proven to be an enigma. Contrary to his admitting physician's report, I'd seen few of the typical signs of manic or hypomanic behavior . . . no hyperactivity, no excessive talking, no hypervigilance. He reported healthy sleep patterns and there had been no mixed or bipolar episodes. His speech was logical and showed no signs of disorganization. In fact, his thoughts were clear and often childlike in their simplicity. He still suffered from acutely elevated self-esteem, the result of his frequent hallucinations, which in turn led to hyper-religiosity, but other than that, and the amnesia resulting from his psychotic break, he was lucid and responsive to those around him.

On a personal note, all the patients liked him. For that matter, so did I, which made me all the more cautious. Between his notoriety and my probation, the Department watched my every move. There would be no infractions with this one. No bending of the rules. I would be the perfect doctor—intolerant of intolerance, dogmatically opposed to dogma.

So, as I had during our other Circle times, I pressed in upon Maxwell. I was sensitive, professional, and firm. Very firm . . .

"Now, correct me if I misunderstood, but are you saying this ethereal being of love that you imagine views everyone as equal?"

He smiled. "No, that's not what I said."

"Oh, then perhaps I misheard."

"Yes you did. God doesn't see any of us as being equal."

Nelson interrupted, "'We hold these truths to be self-evident, that all men are created equal.'"[6]

Maxwell looked at him and nodded. "That may be true with the government, but it's not true with God. We're not equally created . . . but we are equally loved."

"More than God's own life," Bernard said, throwing Maxwell a knowing smile.

Joey nodded. "Good, bad—"

"Genius," Bernard said.

"Or moron," Darcy added for Bernard's benefit. Then, leaning into me, she explained their point. "Love. It ain't something you earn, Doc."

"It is the consequence of being his offspring," Winona said, adjusting her hair, which was a bit neater than usual.

"God is love,"[7] Nelson quoted.

I paused and looked over the group. The purpose of these sessions had always been for others in Circle to take ownership in helping one another. This, in turn, aided in their own recovery. But that's not what had been occurring here. In the short amount of time Maxwell had been with us, *he'd* become the influencing factor. Intentionally or unintentionally, he'd risen as the group leader—an unhealthy sign, given their proclivity toward the religious.

I continued a bit more carefully. "So, if as you say, this supreme being loves everyone equally, then why is there so much inequality?"

He looked at me a moment then glanced away, seeming to drift off in thought.

Darcy shifted in her chair. "Doc's got a point." She ran her hand over her head. "Why are there all them rich people, or good-looking ones, or smart ones. Then you got people like us who are—"

"Losers," Bernard sighed. He was staring across the room at the fire extinguisher again.

I was quick to qualify. "Please, don't misunderstand me. I'm not implying any of you are inferior."

"But it's true," Joseph said. He turned to Maxwell. "Why is that, Max? If he loves us all the same, why do some have it better than others?"

"I hate it 'cause it makes my brain fuzzy!" Chloe exclaimed. She looked around the group and, as was her habit, pulled her hair over her face and slumped back into her chair.

Joseph repeated the question. "If he loves us all the same, why did he make some of us, you know"—he nodded toward Chloe—"the way we are?"

"Misfits," Darcy said.

"Genetic mistakes," Raphael added.

"Abandoned by our mother ship," Winona concluded.

I purposefully waited as, one by one, each member turned to Maxwell for the answer.

Eventually, he spoke. "Do you believe that's what we are? Mistakes?"

No one replied.

He shook his head. "No. I can't believe a loving father would make mistakes."

"Maybe that proves he ain't so loving," Darcy said.

"Maybe," Maxwell said. "Or maybe there's a bigger plan than what we see. Maybe each of us is created the way we are for a very unique and very specific purpose."

Several shifted in their chairs. It appeared they obviously disagreed, and I thought perhaps Maxwell would finally meet some resistance. But after a moment he continued, his voice softer. "From what you've been telling me and from the bits and pieces I remember, I worked in the fashion industry . . . Is that right?"

"Just a little," Darcy smirked.

He continued, once again losing himself in thought. "Sometimes . . . I remember sometimes we would choose fabrics with beautifully woven patterns."

He quit speaking and after several moments I cleared my throat. "Maxwell?"

He blinked. "Sorry. What was I saying?"

"Beautiful fabric with beautiful patterns," Bernard said.

He smiled. "Yes. And sometimes that fabric, those beautiful patterns would have dark, ugly threads running through them." He spread out his hands as if holding a piece of fabric between them. "If you looked too closely," he brought it to his face, "you would wonder, 'Why is this awful, dark thread woven into this beautiful piece of fabric?'"

He paused, having everyone's attention. Then, still staring at the imaginary fabric, he pushed it out to arm's length. "But when you looked at it from a distance, when you saw what the weaver had in mind, you would see that without that thread, there would be no depth. Without that awful, ugly darkness, the fabric would lose its richness, it would lose its beauty." He lowered his hands. "And that's the difference between run-of-the-mill cloth . . . and genius artistry: the use of the ugly threads to create the great masterpiece."

He shook his head as if surprised by his own thoughts. Then he continued. "The question isn't, *WHY* am I created the way I am created. No masterpiece would ever ask that. The question is *HOW*. *HOW* can I use the way I've been woven? *HOW* can I implement it to portray my great beauty? *HOW* can I display it to demonstrate the artist's genius and unfathomable love?"

A quiet awe fell over the group.

"That's beautiful," Bernard whispered.

Winona agreed. "I read something similar on the planet Fayrah—in a children's book."

Max nodded. "Sometimes children's stories have the best insight."

The silence lengthened as a peace settled over us. Well, over them. Because I knew full well where the discussion would lead from here. Conclusions that, as they'd always suspected, they really didn't have mental health issues. That they really didn't need treatment. That the months, in some cases, years of progress in convincing them to stop living a fantasy and face reality, could be jeopardized.

I spoke up. "Maxwell, are you suggesting that those in need should not turn to medical science for help? If a person has a broken arm, should it not be set so it can mend? If we have a mental disorder, should we not try to heal it as well?"

He turned to me, his gaze soft and understanding.

But I would not be deterred. "Are you suggesting that for no apparent reason, people should stop taking their medication?"

"I just told you why," Chloe blurted.

I turned back to her, smiling sadly at the non sequitur.

Maxwell shook his head, "No, of course not."

"Then I'm confused. What exactly are you saying?"

"I'm saying that when it comes to His children, God does not make mistakes. Regardless of how we judge ourselves or others, we are still His children, His creation, and He does not make junk."

I glanced at my watch. Time was up, though we'd obviously have to return to the topic. I was careful not to indicate it, but I was more concerned than ever.

If Maxwell's condition did not improve and if his impact upon the group continued, more aggressive measures would have to be taken. I'd been hesitant to prescribe too much medication, given his lack of manic symptoms, but that would have to change. And if he continued to show no signs of improvement? I didn't like the answer. Sacramento was not my preference, given its severity in approach and treatment, not to mention the horror stories we occasionally heard.

Nevertheless, it may have to be the only course of action—particularly with Junior and the Religious Affairs cronies breathing down my neck. If Maxwell did not show marked improvement, and soon, I would have to recommend his transfer to Sacramento.

Like it or not, it may be in his best interest, as well as the interest of the group. And, though I hated myself for admitting it, it may be in my best interest as well.

twelve

B
E
R
N
A
R
D

I looked over to Max from my new list of mess-ups. Funny, each night I thought I'd covered them all, but after every day I had a few more. "What about thoughts?" I asked. "Should I put down my bad thoughts, too?"

"Sure, why not."

I nodded and stared at my paper. Then, after a moment, I wrote down just one word: "Chloe."

Don't get me wrong, I wasn't having creepy or pervy thoughts about her or anything. But sometimes watching the way she played board games, or ate, or just breathed, I wondered what it would be like to have her as a girlfriend. Actually, more than that. Sometimes I dreamed about her being my wife. And instead of playing Uno in the TV Room, we'd be at home around a cozy fire playing with our children. Lots and lots of children. And they all loved us and called me Poppa, or Poppy, except for, Daphne, the oldest who called me Pops, which wasn't a surprise 'cause she was almost a teenager.

I looked back to Max. "So, how come nobody but us is making lists?"

He looked up from his paper. "I'm sorry?"

"For the Trashman? How come it's just you and me?"

"I don't know. Maybe they forgot."

"Maybe we should remind them."

"That's a thought." He motioned to my left ear. "You, uh, you still have a little something there."

I reached up and pulled a tiny scrap of lasagna from my ear. With a shrug, I popped it into my mouth. We both chuckled, but not like a few hours ago. That's when things were really funny.

It all started with dinner, which is where it kind of ended, too. Actually, it started a little earlier than that, if you count Jamal getting released from Contemplative Lockup. Usually that place helps settle people down when they've been acting out. But not Jamal. Not today. Which was not so great for me.

It was our pod's time for dinner. The hospital has different pods. The one just down the hall, through the electronically locked door, is for drug rehab. Above us are the suicides. Below us the catatonics. Beside them, the criminally insane. Even though we were separated, I guess you could still call us all family.

Anyways, we were moving down the dinner line talking with each other, which also meant Darcy was making her business rounds. I don't think I mentioned, but she hates anything with electricity, which is why she keeps plugging up the outlets in her and Chloe's room—you know, so the electricity doesn't leak out all over the floor. I'm not sure what her official diagnosis is—some sort of worshipper of nature or something. But when it comes to wheeling and dealing in the real world, she knows what she's doing. She heard they were stepping up Max's meds so she was in front of me working on him to get more. Not all of them. That would get her in trouble. Usually she just goes for, like, one out of every three or four. At least that's her rule with everybody else. For me she usually winds up getting them all 'cause I like being so helpful.

Anyways, everyone's standing in the food line having their conversations— Ralphy and Joey, Darcy and Max, Nelson and himself, and Darcy's tattoos and me . . .

"Don't look now, idiot child," One Eye was saying, "'less, of course, you want to know who's 'bout to destroy you."

"Destroy me?" I asked.

"Maybe he don't want to know," the other head said. "Sometimes ignorance is bliss."

"Or in his case, reality."

"Better ignorant than ugly."

"Who said he ain't ugly?"

Talk about hate speech. If anyone needed medication, those two did. I was about to make that suggestion—politely, of course—when I noticed how quiet the room got. And how everybody was looking in my direction, kind of sad and worried. I soon discovered the reason.

"You're standing in my spot, road kill."

I turned and there he was. "Oh, hi, Jamal. You're out, I see. How was your stay?"

He glared down at me.

I smiled up at him.

Without a word, and never taking his eyes from mine, he reached out and grabbed my food tray.

"Oh, sure, help yourself," I said. "I think you'll find the cooked spinach especially tasty this evening."

"It's Caesar salad," Winona said from behind the serving counter.

I turned to her. "Caesar salad?"

She nodded. "Aged to perfection."

"I see. Well, maybe Jamal would—"

"Shut up." It was more growl than words.

"Oh, sorry," I said. "Good point. You probably have a lot on your mind. I wouldn't want to disturb your thinking." I reached up to the dessert shelf. "Here, why don't you have my peach cobbler, too."

"Tapioca pudding," Winona said.

"Right." I handed him the bowl. "Since I'm not having dinner I really don't need dessert. So why don't you—"

Up to that point we were making pretty good progress in what Dr. Aadil calls "interpersonal reconciliation." Communication lines were open, gifts were being exchanged. Of course we might have made better progress if Jamal hadn't raised his hand to stop me. And it might have helped if I had noticed the gesture. The good news was the bowl of tapioca stopped when it hit his hand. The bad news was the tapioca didn't. It just sort of kept going, leaping out of the bowl, flying through the air, and landing directly on the front of his very black, very expensive, silk shirt.

I kind of went cold inside. I didn't know what to do. So I just giggled nervously as I watched it ooze down the front of his very expensive, once very black, silk shirt.

He watched too, but without the giggling. When he looked back to me, my life suddenly flashed before my eyes. Well, not really. Mostly just the death part, which I guess was sort of a preparation thing. I looked over to Biff (or was it Britt?) hoping he'd come to my rescue. Unfortunately, Britt (or was it Biff?) was too busy flirting with Chloe to notice.

But not Max. "Hey, Bernie," he said. "Are you stupid or what?"

My heart kind of sank. I knew Max liked truth and everything, but it would have been nice to hear something a little more positive, especially before I died. When I turned to him to point this out, I (SPLAT) suddenly got a bowl full of chili in my face. I blinked and wiped away the beans to see Max grinning. Of course my heart sank even lower. Why would he do such a thing? I thought we were friends, I thought—

And then I heard it: a little chortle. Barely discernible at first. But when I turned back to Jamal he was smiling (or snarling . . . it's hard to tell the difference). Either way the chortle grew into a chuckle and the snarl/smile grew into a grin, so big you could see the ginormous gap between his teeth.

"Hey, Max?" another voice called.

Max turned just in time to see a gooey slab of lasagna flying at him, courtesy of Winona. He managed to duck. I (*SPLAT*) didn't. Now I wore two coats of dinner on my face . . . which, for some reason, turned Jamal's chuckle into laughter, until—

"Hey, Jamal!"

He turned and (*SPLAT*) he was suddenly covered with creamed spinach/Caesar salad, courtesy of Darcy. He stood there, stunned. Then he blinked.

A hush fell over the room. Then, ever so slowly, his grin reappeared through the greens. In one swift move, he grabbed a vegetarian plate from the rack, and before Darcy could duck, she (*SPLAT*) got a face full of low-cholesterol, health food.

Laughing, she grabbed the creamed corn (or boiled cauliflower) off her tray and threw it at him, to which he ducked, to which I ducked, to which (*SPLAT*) Winona didn't.

And so it began. Soon, all the pod joined in.

"In war there is no substitute for victory!"[8] Nelson shouted as people flung every imaginable entrée in every imaginable direction into every imaginable face. The four basic food groups were everywhere—the walls, the floors, our clothes, our hair.

"Take no prisoners!"[9]

Everybody laughed and slipped and slid on the slick floor, which grew slicker with every course.

It's true, we might have gotten a little carried away, especially when Jamal and Britt (or was it Biff?) picked up a giant vat of soup and dumped it on top of Biff's (or was it Britt's) head. It made us all double over with laughter so hard we couldn't catch our breaths as we dropped to the floor, still flinging and slinging. Seriously, it was the funniest thing I'd ever seen.

But the guys watching upstairs in Video Surveillance didn't think so, which explains why they brought in Security from a couple of the other pods to practice their Taser skills. That part wasn't so great, but the rest was wonderful. Because for that one moment in time, we were all little children again—every one of us laughing and playing just like we were kids.

That had been three hours ago. And, like little children, we'd all been sent to our rooms without supper (except for what we could pick off our bodies and out of our clothes). Now, me and Max sat in our room, killing time, making our lists—which, for obvious reasons, were just a little longer.

Eventually there was a knock on the door. I got up and opened it and there was Trashman, smiling away like he did every evening about this time.

"Hi," I said, "come on in."

He nodded and wheeled his squeaking cart inside.

"Ah, amigo . . ." Max rose from his desk. "Buenas noches."

Trashman grinned. "Buenas noches." They shook hands and shared a brief hug. "Cómo estás?"

"Bien, bien, gracias."

When they finished, Max crossed back to his desk. He tore off the list from his notebook, crumpled it up, and tossed it into the trash bag.

Trashman nodded with a grin.

I crumpled up my own list and tossed it in. "Have there been any others?" I asked.

He looked up at me.

"Lists for the trash." I motioned to the bag and spoke slower and louder, so he could understand. "HAS . . . ANYBODY . . . ELSE . . . GIVEN . . ." I motioned to him. "YOU?"

He broke into another smile and shook his head. "No, no."

I looked to Max who began nodding to me. "Maybe you're right. Maybe they need a little reminder."

I agreed. "We can tell them again at Circle tomorrow"

Trashman shrugged, then looked to Max. Neither of them spoke, but it was almost like they knew what the other was thinking. The little Mexican began to smile. So did Max.

"Or . . ." Max started for the closet.

"Or what?"

He reached in and pulled out his nice flannel robe. Thankfully it was the white one without all those chattering patterns. "Or we can remind them tonight." He slipped it on and turned to Trashman. "Would you mind? If we knocked on their doors and spoke to them tonight?"

Trashman's smile turned to a grin. "Bueno. Bueno."

"It's still early, we've got plenty of time."

"Sí." Trashman nodded. "Ándale." He grabbed his cart and started for the door.

Max followed.

"No, wait," I said. "You can't do that."

"Why not?"

"They sent us to our rooms. Without dinner."

"We're not going to eat."

"I know, but what if they—" I swallowed and glanced up to the video camera. "What if they don't want us to visit each other?"

"Did they say that?"

"Well, no. But what if you're wrong?"

"There's only one way to find out." He opened the door. "You coming?"

"Max . . ."

He turned back to me. Now it was *our* turn to talk without words. Finally, he said, "Bernie, you don't have to be afraid. There's nothing wrong with being wrong."

I frowned.

"That's how we learn."

"Right. But . . ."

He opened the door wider and looked back at me. "Sometimes the fear of being wrong is worse than actually being wrong."

I wanted to answer but I wasn't sure what to say. I mean he made sense and everything and I wanted to go. But I couldn't.

He smiled, then quietly answered, "It's okay, you don't need to come. It's all right."

"Really?"

"Really." I could tell by the kindness in his eyes that he meant it. "Just keep the door unlocked. We'll be back before you know it."

The two of them stepped into the hallway.

"But, why . . . ?"

He turned back to me.

"Why do you have to do it tonight? Why don't you just wait and tell them tomorrow?"

He thought a moment. "I guess I could. But I like them, Bernie. I really like them."

I frowned some more.

"And the sooner they write out their stuff and get rid of it, the sooner they'll have room for God's."

thirteen

B
E
R
N
A
R
D

I was pretty worried about Max. Biff (or was it Britt?) had already stuck his head into the room giving us the thirty-minute warning. I told him Max was in the bathroom. (Okay, so I'd add that to tomorrow's list).

Anyways, it was close to Lights Out and he still wasn't back. A couple times I opened the door a crack to take a peek up and down the hall, but he wasn't there. I figured he and Trashman were in somebody's room. Of course, I could run up and down the hall knocking on everyone's doors until I found him, but with my luck I'd be the one who got caught.

So, even though I hated myself, which isn't too hard to do, I climbed into bed, turned off the lights, and tried to go to sleep. Pretty soon, before I knew it, I was back on that hillside chatting away with my not-so-little and not-so-nice, boulder buddies.

"Might as well get comfy, nutcase," the one just above my head sneered. "You're gonna be here a long time."

"Can we get you anything?" the one over my legs said. "Scorpions, fire ants? Black widows are popular this time of year."

"I've got a lovely nest of rattlers over here," another said.

I responded the only way I knew how. "MAX!"

But he still wouldn't help. "Listen to the music," he kept shouting. "Listen to the music."

Okay, enough was enough. I'd been as polite to the boulders as I knew how to be. Now I had to get tough. No more Mr. Nice Guy. I reached up to the one above my head and began feeling around for a good handhold.

"Please," he giggled, "we've barely met."

"At least buy him dinner," another said.

I finally found a good place and pushed with all my strength. He barely budged an inch.

"Really?" he taunted, "that's all you got?"

I gave up and tried pushing the one above my chest.

"Hee-hee, that tickles."

"The music, Bernie!" Max shouted. "Focus on the music!"

I tried the third one over my waist.

"Keep that up and I'm filing for sexual harassment."

"Bernie!"

Like I said before, the nice thing about inanimate objects is, if you really work at it, you can ignore them. So I closed my eyes and forced everything out of my head . . . except for the music. But like I also said, the song was so faint and breathy it wasn't always easy to hear. So, to help, I tried humming along—you know, filling in the gaps where the notes should be.

"That's it," Max shouted. "Use the music."

I reached up to the first rock. I'm sure he was saying something rude, but his words had gotten fainter because of the music and my humming. I pushed harder. I hummed louder, almost shouting like those weight lifters do when they lift heavy weights. And you know something? It worked. I actually started moving the boulder.

"That's it, Bernie. Keep it up!"

I kept pushing and humming and it kept moving . . . until it finally rolled away to the side. The sun poured in and I had to wince. But that was okay. I reached for the boulder over my chest.

"What are you doing?" he shouted. "You can't do this!"

I hummed even louder and pushed with everything I had until, sure enough, he also rolled to the side, slamming into the first one, who showed his appreciation with some major bad language. But I barely heard. I just kept focusing on the music and my humming.

I reached for the rock over my hips. He was easily twice the size of the first, but it didn't make any difference. In fact he was actually lighter as he cried and pleaded until I finally rolled him away. Then I pushed aside the next rock. And the next. Until, at last, I could climb out of the gully and stagger to my feet.

"Atta boy, Bernie!"

I looked up the hill, shading my eyes against the sun. And there was Max, still dancing. And Trashman, still playing.

"Stack them on top of each other!" Max shouted.

"What?"

"Like a monument, like an altar. Make an altar out of them so you can remember."

"They're just rocks."

"Trust me," Max shouted. "If not for you, then for others."

Since I knew I was dreaming and since it was kind of fun being like Superman with all that strength, I figured, why not. So, even though the rocks hollered and swore, I just kept humming and picking up one after another and tossing them onto a pile.

"Atta boy!" Max kept laughing and clapping until I was done. Then he motioned and shouted, "Come on up."

I gave the pile one last look before turning and starting back up the hill. It was still hard going but I was feeling pretty good, and the music and humming really helped. I was only a step or two from the top when Max reached down and pulled me the rest of the way.

"Nice work, Bernie." He gave me a hug. "We're really proud of you."

Trashman nodded and smiled as he kept playing.

"Take a look around." Max motioned to the countryside. "Have you ever seen anything more beautiful?"

He was right. The foothills around us were so bright and green they actually shimmered. Below them and to my right was a wheat field that stretched to some giant, snow covered mountains that had great, jagged peaks and a waterfall I could hear roaring even from where we stood. Below and to my left was a huge field of golden dandelions, which I know are supposed to be weeds, but even they were beautiful. And beyond them were sunflowers. Oh, and a couple hills over from us was a rainbow-colored bridge-like thing, so wispy and misty you could barely see it. It arched across the valley, all the way to the mountains.

"Wow," was all I could say.

"Yeah." Max grinned.

"This is some dream."

"It's more than a dream, Bernie. And we're going to be exploring it."

"Now?"

"Soon. Until then"—he motioned to Trashman— "dance with us."

"But . . . I don't know how to dance."

"Of course you do."

I shook my head, embarrassed even at the thought.

"You're already tapping your foot."

He was right, I was. But that wasn't the same as—

"So, instead of your foot, tap your whole body." He began to sway. "Let your whole body move to the music."

I stood, kind of paralyzed, feeling my face getting hot.

"Come on. No one's watching." He swayed even more until he took a step forward and then backward.

"I . . . I can't."

"What? You can move giant boulders, but you can't move your feet? Come on, give it a try."

I looked down at my shoes.

"Come on, Bernie."

I lifted my right foot. It felt almost as heavy as those boulders. Then I set it down.

"That's right."

I did the same with my left.

"Great."

"Really?"

He nodded.

I tried again. Right foot up and down. Left foot up and down.

"Now let your whole body join in."

I did it again—foot up, foot down, only this time I also swayed a little.

"That's right, you're getting it. Feel the music. Let it get inside you."

I did it again. Foot up, foot down. Then again. I looked up at him, grinning.

He grinned back. "That's it."

I wasn't sure I was getting any better, but I was starting to feel it. Well, feel something.

"All right!" Max began to laugh. "Shake your booty, Bernie. Let yourself go."

I wasn't sure what he was talking about but I started laughing with him. I don't know how long this went on, swaying back and forth (I might have even done a tiny bit of jumping up and down, who knows). All I know is that when I woke up in the morning, I felt happier than I had in a very, very long time.

fourteen

A
L
E
X
I
S

When Robert slipped into my office I was studying my mood board—that big piece of whiteboard we stick anything and everything on to inspire creativity—fabric swatches, photos, torn out magazine articles, jewelry. Last year I specialized in shag carpeting.

"So how's it going, Pudge?" Which, for the record, is a name he never uses in public, unless he plans on forgoing any future use of his reproductive faculties.

I squinted past the board as he entered (Robert never walks in, he enters)—his three-piece suit so precisely fitted and tailored you'd think he was gay. Unfortunately, that's not the case. As embarrassing as it is, you get a few gin and tonics in him and he'll fess up that he's straight—which, of course, is another reason he'll never get ahead in the industry. Gays are the ones with taste, better than most women. Truth be told, next to teen girls, no one understands the fashion scene better.

"Pretty early," he said. "Been up all night?"

"Maybe. Probably. I guess."

"Making any progress?"

"You bet."

"Really?"

"Really." I took a drag from my menthol cig and blew it toward the ceiling fan. "It's going great."

"You've got nothing, do you."

"Not a thing."

He'd crossed around my desk until he could see the board.

"Dental floss?" He tried to hide his incredulity.

"And their containers." I pointed to the twenty different packets glued to the board. It looked like one of those air traffic control maps with lines shooting out at different angles from the different packets, all crisscrossing one another.

He stepped closer. "I didn't know they made so many different kinds."

"Oh yeah." I took another drag and blew it at the ceiling. "Waxed, unwaxed, white, blue, braided white and blue, peppermint, cinnamon, they even have it flattened into tape—see, here?"

He leaned in. "Amazing."

"Yeah," I said.

"Yeah," he agreed.

We continued to stare. No sound but the faint bubbling of my giant, built-in aquarium. Saltwater fish are beautiful creatures, arrayed in shimmering greens, blues, reds, silvers, and violets. Of course I'd never taken time to name any since their life-span in my capable hands ranged between five and eight days.

I broke the silence and nodded toward the studio door that my new staff hid behind, pretending to earn their pay. "How are the children?"

"So young. When we go out I'm never sure whether to buy them drinks or cans of Simalac. I'm twenty-nine and I feel like an old man."

"You're thirty-one. You are old. So what are they doing?"

"Just trying to stay occupied, waiting for your vision."

"Yeah," I said.

"Yeah," he said.

We stared at the board.

"Hard designing accessories if they don't know what to accessorize."

I nodded. "Glad it's only a three-hundred billion dollar industry or I'd feel some pressure."

"Yeah," he said.

"Yeah," I said.

"Got a call from *VOGUE* last night."

"And?"

"We're getting the December cover."

"Fantastic," I said.

"Yeah, fantastic."

"Are they going to get us real models this time or do we have to use their Hollywood chubbos?"

"I thought we liked Hollywood?"

"Only the famous."

"Like Vittoria Haven?"

"Like Vittoria Haven."

Robert stretched and cracked his neck, sounding like a bowl of Rice Krispies. "Any news on Troy?" he asked.

"Besides texting me every hour?"

"You're kidding."

I raised a knowing eyebrow.

"Sweet."

I nodded then returned to topic. "What about the models? Are they dishing out any cash for the 'A' list?"

"Let's just say their air brush department is going to be busy."

I swore, shaking my head.

He nodded, then as delicately as possible added, "Of course, we'll still need something to put them in."

"Robert, I know."

"I'm just saying—"

"I know what you're saying. I know what everybody's saying, all right. It'll happen. Just give me a little time, it will happen."

"The shoot's in twenty-nine days. New York is eleven weeks."

"I said, it will happen!"

"All right, Pudge, all right." He kissed the top of my head and started for the door. "Oh, you know you got a call from the hospital, right?"

"I haven't been picking up." We both threw a look to the fish tank where, on bad days, my cell phones practice their deep sea diving. "Is he all right?"

"Didn't sound urgent. The doc just thought a little more connecting might do him some good."

"In all my spare time?"

"In all your spare time."

I pulled out another cigarette, lit it with the remains of the other, and turned back to the board.

"You know, we can always go retro."

I gave him a look reserved for peeling skin off faces. Fashion repeats itself every twenty years or so. Worst-case scenario, if you can't think of something original, go back and reintroduce some twenty-year-old look. It's a cheat and considered the bane of the industry . . . which explains why fashion runs in twenty-year cycles.

"Tootles," he said, as he turned and gently closed the door behind him.

I butted out the old cig and took a long drag from the new.

fifteen

B
E
R
N
A
R
D

"Please, please don't eat me! I beg you!"

I scowled hard at my plate.

"You've still got the bacon. And what about that toast?"

I felt pretty bad for the egg yolk. But the truth is, I'd already eaten all the white around it, and this morning's toast was a bit more cremated than usual, and since I'm trying to swear off meat to impress Chloe, it's not like I had much choice.

"Please, I beg you. Please, please!"

Deciding I could at least give it a brief stay of execution I turned to listen to Darcy and the others talk about last night.

"You're telling me *ALL* you morons made out lists?" Darcy said.

"You did not?" Ralphy asked.

"Not me and not Chloe, no way."

I turned to Chloe who was also making up her mind about the toast.

"Why not?" Ralphy asked.

"Because it's stupid," Darcy said. "Believing in something you can't see is plain stupid."

"And yet," Ralphy said, "do you not believe in nature?"

"I can see nature. Grass, plants, trees—why wouldn't I believe in that stuff?"

"You only believe in what you can see?"

"Or touch or hear or smell, yeah."

"Congratulations, Earthling." Winona had fashioned a new pair of aluminum foil cuffs for her wrists. "That means you only believe in six percent of reality."

Darcy gave her a look. "What's that supposed to mean?"

"It means the scientists of your world are unable to identify ninety-four percent of reality. Whatever the other stuff is cannot be observed so they've invented ignorant names for it like Dark Matter and Dark Energy."

Darcy turned to Joey. "Is that true?"

Joey nodded.

"So if you only believe in the quantifiable, you only believe in six percent of reality." She took a drink of orange juice/orange water and stifled a burp. "Then there are the nineteen additional dimensions believed to exist outside your current three dimensions, and . . . well, don't get me started."

"Okay, we won't," Darcy muttered.

Of course I was completely lost about what they were talking about. But I wasn't lost on what she'd said about Chloe. That's why I leaned over and asked, "Is it true? You really didn't make out a list?"

She shrugged.

"Why not?"

Another shrug.

"It's not that scary," I said. "Actually, it can be kind of funny. Sometimes it makes me laugh and shake my head over how foolish I've been."

Nelson stared up at the ceiling. "The average four-year-old laughs three hundred times a day, a forty-year-old, laughs four."[10]

"What about people like Jamal?" Darcy asked. "Can he make out a list, too?"

"Sure," Max said.

Ralphy adjusted his shower cap. "Señor Max, the man, he does not exactly play by the rules."

Max turned to him. "It's not about rules, Ralphy. Remember? It's about relationship. If I love someone enough, I'll just naturally try and do what's best for the relationship. It's love that changes us. Not rules."

"So knowing the rules of God, that is not enough?"

"Sometimes it's just the opposite. Sometimes knowing good and evil is *TOO* much."

Nelson quoted, "You must not eat from the tree of the knowledge of good and evil, for when you eat of it you will surely die."[11]

Max continued. "But if we just know Him, if all we do is experience Him to our core . . . that's more than we'll ever need."

We all sat kind of quiet until Joey finally asked, "But how do we do that? Experience Him, I mean?"

Max nodded like it was a good question. Then he answered, "Most of the time I have to get very quiet."

"Like not talking," I said.

"No, quieter than that, Bernie. I have to go someplace like my room or out in the courtyard, away from all the distractions. And then I just sit there and quiet my soul."

"Soul?" Winona asked.

"Who I am, inside—my thoughts, my emotions. I just sit there letting them grow still—sometimes ten minutes, sometimes an hour, just sitting there, thinking of Him."

"Be still and know that I am God,"[12] Nelson quoted.

"Good luck," Joey said. "Keeping my mind still for ten seconds would be a miracle."

"It is true," Ralphy agreed. "My thoughts, they are always scampering like little ants inside my head."

"And that's okay," Max said. "When other thoughts come in, I don't push them away, I try to include them. I think how they can also be examples of His greatness."

"So you're not just making your mind go blank," Joey said. "You're thinking of God."

"Yes. I'm dwelling on His goodness, His beauty."

"I do that," Darcy argued. "When I commune with nature."

"And that's a good start," Max said. "But why commune with a single book, when you can commune with the Author of the entire library?"

Things got real quiet again. I hated to break the mood, but I had to ask. "But . . . what if we're not, you know, good enough?"

"Good enough to talk to God," Joey said.

Winona answered, "That is the purpose of the list, to ensure we are."

"But sometimes," I said, "I still don't feel like I deserve it. Sometimes I keep doing the same stuff over and over again."

Max nodded. "Me, too. And those are the times I have to simply trust what Trashman is doing. Whether it makes sense or not. Like a little child, I just have to believe."

Nelson quoted, "Anyone who will not receive the kingdom of God like a little child will never enter it."[13]

Max gave another nod. "And once we enter it, well that's when the adventure really begins."

"Enter heaven?" Joey grabbed his chair. "I'm too young to die!"

Max chuckled. "No, not that heaven. The one we're getting ready to step into. Any day now."

Everyone traded some pretty nervous glances.

Max explained. "What Trashman is doing for us is just the beginning. Not the end, the beginning. And it's going to be a fantastic journey."

Nobody said anything more. Not that I blamed them. Things were way too confusing. I looked back down to my plate. The egg had gotten real quiet, too. Probably playing possum. So, before it had a chance to start begging again, I slipped my fork under it, plopped the whole yoke into my mouth, and squished it. There was no screaming, no pleas for mercy, just the thick, wonderful gooeyness filling my mouth. If this was all heaven was, it would be enough.

sixteen

D
R

A
A
D
I
L

"Let's go, folks, times a-wasting." I turned to Raphael who stood outside with me at the mini-bus door, hands on hips, carefully surveying the parking lot. "You, too, Raphael."

"If you don't mind, I shall assist until all our charges are safely on board."

Darcy marched up the steps between us. "It's Tues-day, twerp. Arch villains never show up on Tuesdays."

Raphael frowned and looked to me. Joseph started up the steps behind her and I reached out to steady him. "She has a point. It is Tuesday."

Raphael thought a moment, then gallantly flipped his bath towel to the side. "They are a tricky lot, Doctor. Raphael Montoya Hernandez III shall stay to defend until the very end."

"All right." I took Chloe's hand and helped her onto the bus. But when she reached the top step, she spun around and shouted at the parking lot, "Run!"

I waited patiently until she looked at me. As always, she was embarrassed over her outburst. I smiled and nodded for her to join the others onboard. As she turned to obey, I glanced at my watch. 1:40 PM. We were running a little late for Tuesday's field trip to the soup kitchen in the Tenderloin. Nevertheless, the staff had assured me we'd be gone well before they transported Jamal. That's how patients were removed—waiting for their fellow patients to be gone to create as little anxiety as possible.

This morning had not been easy. I'd been upstairs in the administrator's office all morning presenting Jamal's case to my newly assigned keepers: three physicians—an ambitious thirty-something beauty with long legs she was not adverse to exploiting, an older Dr. Middleton whose mid-life crises fixated upon those legs, and Chief Physician, Dr. Hague, head of the entire hospital.

We sat around his mahogany desk overflowing with so many papers that for no apparent reason stacks would suddenly cascade to the floor.

"You must understand," I'd said. "Jamal Brown was simply in the wrong place at the wrong time."

As with his attack on . . ." Hague flipped through the papers in his folder to read, "Bernard Goldstein?"

"A misunderstanding."

"And several months ago when Ms. Darcy Hamilton was provoked to break his nose?"

She was merely establishing boundaries.

"I see. Then we have last month's altercation with orderly, Britton Samuels?"

"It was an argument, nothing more. Britton Samuels has clearly shown prejudice toward those with Islamic leanings. I've written him up. Surely you've read the report."

"Speaking of which . . ."

I turned to Middleton who had torn his gaze from Thirty-Something's legs long enough to remove his glasses and tap their frame sagely against his folder.

"I wonder . . . could this vigorous defense on Mr. Brown's behalf have anything to do with your own religious background?"

The accusation brought a stunned silence to the room. Thirty-Something shifted her body away from his, indicating his mid-life crisis would no doubt remain in crises.

I, on the other hand, kept my voice cool and professional. "I do not embrace my religious heritage any more than you do, Doctor . . . given that it inflicted nearly as much pain and suffering as did your—what was it again, Catholic, or was it Protestant?—ancestors during the Crusades, Inquisition, Reformation and witch hunts."

He replaced his glasses and resumed studying his folder.

"Dr. Aadil."

I turned back to Hague.

"In his eight-month stay, Jamal Brown has shown virtually no sign of improvement. And according to the records, his actions have actually proved a hindrance to others in the program."

"Still, he is making progress," I said. "Not at the rate we hoped, but his attitude and occasional outbursts stem more from a socio-economic environment than any opposition to our treat—"

"Doctor." It was Middleton again. "According to your own file, the man is a risk, not only to himself, but to staff members, as well as to the other patients."

I caught a glimpse of Hague nodding. Thirty-Something joined in, once she knew which way the wind was blowing.

Hague sighed. "I'm afraid Dr. Middleton is right."

More nodding, a little throat clearing, and some leg re-crossing.

Finally Hague asked, "We are in agreement, then? It is this committee's decision that Jamal Brown be transferred to the Sacramento Center of Religious Rehabilitation?"

"Aye," Middleton said.

Thirty-Something nodded.

I gave no answer, which didn't matter. One of the perks of being on probation.

"Right then." Hague closed the file and reached for another. "Now, about Maxwell Portenelli."

"Wait a minute, hold on," I said. "There have been no incidents with—"

"We've read your notes, Doctor."

"Right, but—"

"And, we have conversations recorded outside Circle by one of your patients."

I turned to Middleton. "You what? Someone is recording—"

"He is a high profile case."

"Then, of course, there are the videos from Surveillance," Thirty-Something said.

I turned to her, then to Hague.

He answered. "Not only is your patient violating curfew, he is actually visiting other patients, and proselytizing them.

"You're not serious?"

"And with a fair amount of success."

Middleton added, "You really should start paying more attention to your patients, Doctor."

"Not if it means spying on them, infringing upon their privacy!"

He countered cool and calm. "There is no privacy here, Doctor. It is a State facility."

"Maxwell Portenelli is not a threat."

"You yourself wrote," Middleton looked down to his folder and read, "'He is very persuasive and the patients are quite intrigued by his religious arguments.'"

"Yes, but all he does is speak about a god of love."

"For now," Hague said, "But it will soon turn."

Middleton nodded. "It always turns."

I looked from one face to the other. "You would ship him off, too?"

"Portenelli is a public figure," Hague said. "We don't need the added publicity. If there is difficulty, the sooner we transfer him to another facility, the better."

"You're not suggesting we ship two patients off at the same time?"

Hague shook his head. "No. That would be too much trauma for the others. What we are suggesting is that you keep an eye on him, Doctor. A very close eye."

"Because we are," Middleton said.

Hague slowly nodded. Which, of course, meant Thirty-Something nodded.

Raphael's voice brought me back to the bus. "Okay, Doctor, that's everyone."

"Good. Thanks, Raphael."

"It is always a pleasure to serve, Doctor."

I motioned for him to get on board and followed. But I'd barely taken the first step before I heard the commotion at the loading dock—a door slamming, scuffling feet, the shouting of oaths.

I turned to see Jamal emerge from the shadows, his hands bound in wrist restraints and two large men on either side. They half-accompanied, half-dragged him down the steps to a white, nondescript, SUV. Had I been more alert I would have noticed the vehicle earlier. Had Security displayed a glimmer of intelligence they would have followed instructions and waited until my patients left the grounds.

Bernard was the first to shout. "Jamal!"

Jamal resisted with every step, twisting, fighting, swearing. I was surprised they had not sedated him. Maybe they had.

"Jamal!" Darcy lowered her window. Others joined her. "They're taking Jamal!"

Suddenly he raised his right elbow and, spinning around, struck one of the escorts in the face. Using surprise to his advantage, he broke free and ran. He stumbled, nearly lost his balance, but continued, racing toward the open gate some eighty yards away.

The patients began cheering. "Go Jamal! Run! Run!"

And run he did. He sprinted toward the gate like an Olympic champion.

"That a boy, Jamal!" they shouted. "Run!"

I turned back to Raphael who remained standing on the top step. "Inside! Raphael, everyone inside the bus."

If he heard, he gave no indication.

"Go Jamal!"

The escorts pursued, the bigger one shouting, "Shut the gate! Shut the gate!"

Jamal was forty yards from freedom, running with everything he had.

"Go, Jamal! Go!"

The hurricane fence, topped with razor wire, began sliding shut. But it was too slow. Jamal would easily make it. We saw it. So did the gatekeeper. The gray-haired fool was nearly as old as me, but it didn't stop him from trying to be a hero. He had hobbled from the guard shack and was shouting, "Stop! Stop right there!"

Jamal showed little interest in obeying. He'd outdistanced his pursuers with every step, gasping like a racehorse, his freedom just yards ahead . . . until the guard pulled a side arm from his holster.

"No!" Darcy shouted. "Jamal!"

The others joined her. They had no way of knowing the guard was only armed with pepper spray and a revolver that fired rubber bullets. But it was a revolver that looked like any other.

"Jamal!"

"I order you to stop!"

But Jamal did not stop.

"No!" Darcy shouted. "Don't—"

Jamal was ten feet away when the guard fired. Two rounds. They struck him in the chest with such force that he staggered and fell to the ground.

"No!" Darcy cried.

"They shot him!" Winona shouted.

"He's dead!" others joined in. "He's dead! They killed him!"

But of course he wasn't dead. Still, it didn't prevent the horror or the trauma, as they watched the big aides arrive and brutally yank Jamal to his feet.

No, Jamal Brown wasn't dead. I would explain to the group what had happened. But with the violence they'd just witnessed, along with the ever-present rumors of Sacramento, I'm sure they thought much, if not most, of his life was already over.

seventeen

S
A
F
F
R
O
N

So me and Brandylin, we go up to the soup kitchen on Eddy Street. Not a favorite place to take my baby, 'specially with all them nasty men, and her lookin' so fine, but we do what we got to. Also, I ain't crazy 'cause it's startin' to be a hangout for gang bangers, and with JJ and Mariposa off recyclin', we all by ourselves. I don't like it, but we do what we got to.

On the way over we swing by the lady's room at McD's to freshen up. But they're outta soap. How we s'pposed to maintain our high standards of personal hygiene if they got no soap? Course J Box up the street probably got plenty, but they make you ask for the key and most of the staff know me by now, so that ain't good.

All that to say, my 'tude ain't the best when we finally show up and stand in line with fellow indigenous types—old and older, dead and deader—trying to focus on the smell of food and not our neighbor. We're shufflin' down the line gettin' our spaghetti, watery soup, mashed potatoes, which are also watery, and bread. I nod to Brandylin and she stuffs a couple extra breads into her coat 'til some bald server with dragon tats all over her arm gives her a look. But when she turns away, Brandylin grabs more. Like I said, she knows her way 'round.

I get my spaghetti from some big, dough-faced volunteer who says to me, "Good afternoon, Your Highness."

I let it go, thinkin' it's just his way of makin' a joke. But he keeps at it. "And how is your kingdom today?"

Now it's obvious he's makin' fun, and like I said, I ain't in the mood, so I says, "You comin' on to me?"

He blinks them big, brown eyes at me and stutters, "Sorry?"

I see he's some mental, probably a virgin with stacks of porn under his bed, so I push in for some fun of my own. "You wanna roll?" I say. "That what you askin' me?"

More blinkin'. "No, no. I'm sorry, I meant no harm. It's just . . ."

"Jus' what?"

"Your robe."

"My what?"

He nods to my sweatshirt. "Your robe. It's telling me you are—" He takes a breath like he's afraid a what he's gonna say.

"What?" I say.

"It's telling me that you are . . . royalty."

I frown. So he *IS* makin' fun.

And he keeps goin'. "So I just naturally thought, I mean, I figured—"

"Hey, Bernie." Some trim, middle-aged type that's all smiles and with real kind eyes steps in. "Everything okay?"

Dough Face looks relieved. "Oh, hi, Max. I was just telling this lovely lady—"

"He wants to do the nasty with me."

Them kind eyes turn to him. "Really?"

The kid's face gets all red. "No," he sputters, "that's not, that's not what I meant. Not at all."

"You callin' me a liar?" I say.

More sputtering.

That's when I suddenly remember. This place, it's more than jus' a kitchen. It's got rooms upstairs. If me and Brandylin make a big enough stink, like we really offended, like we might report them for hate speech, we might score a nice, warm cot for the night. I could use a nice warm cot, 'specially with all the drizzle of late, so I raise my voice real loud so everyone hears. "No one calls me a liar. I got respect. I'm a respected person. Just 'cause I'm poor, don't mean I don't got respect!"

Kind Eyes tries calmin' me. "Ma'am—"

I get louder. "This boy here," I turn to the others behind me. "He thinks I some crack-whore!" Now I got everyone's attention. "Just 'cause I got me some bad luck he thinks I'm a clucker."

"Ma'am, nobody's calling you an addict or a prostitute."

I turn back. "Good, 'cause I—"

"You do a line from time to time, but that's only to relieve the stress from your daughter and boyfriend."

I look at him surprised. "I what?"

"And the prostitution. It's good you want to stop. Trying to support your man's habit is understandable, but you're both called to something much great—"

"What you know 'bout me, 'bout my man? You don't know nothin'!"

"Actually, that's not true."

"What—"

"I know you're loved . . . more than you can imagine."

I try lookin' away, but them eyes, it's like they're holdin' me.

"You were just a little girl. You have to stop blaming yourself for your stepfather's actions."

My mouth opens then shuts. And I keep starin' at them eyes, feelin' myself gettin' dragged in. But not without a fight. "Who do—" I clear my voice and go again. "Who do you think you are, tellin' me—"

"Is there a problem?" Some old Arab type, in a sweater and tie, sticks his face in.

I shout, "These men are dissin' me!"

"It's . . . it's not true," Dough Face stutters.

"See. They call me a liar."

"My mother is not a liar." Brandylin's voice is quiverin'. She ain't sure what I'm doin' but like I says she's got twice the street smarts of any her age.

"She's a thief!" Suddenly another server, some Asian chick, gets into the act. She's pointin' right at Brandylin.

I give her a glare. "What you call my kid?"

The Arab, old-timer wraps an arm around the chick like he's her uncle or somethin'. "She didn't mean anything. Sometimes Chloe is—"

"Yes, I did. She stole Winona's bracelet." The chick motions down the line to the soup server, another nutjob in white hair and aluminum foil 'round her neck and wrists.

I turn to the Arab and shout, "You the manager?"

"No," he says, "but I'm in charge of this group and I assure you—"

"I want the manager!"

The Asian chick repeats, "She stole Winona's bracelet."

"Chloe," White Hair whispers.

"It's gone." The chick motions to White Hair's wrist. "Show them."

"I want the manager!"

Brandylin shouts, "My mother wants the manager!"

I turn back to the crowd, keepin' the show goin'. "Where's the manager?"

"Show them," the Asian chick keeps sayin'. "Show them your wrist."

White Hair reaches to the counter beside her and picks up a bracelet with little cats jangling on it. "I removed its presence, so as not to contaminate the soup."

"Where's the manager?" I keep shouting. "I want an apology!"

Brandylin kicks it higher, pretendin' to get all hysterical. "My mother is not a liar!"

"My daughter is no thief!"

"Nobody is implying—"

"Where's the manager?"

Brandylin breaks down, sobbing. "My mother is not a crack whore! She's a good person!"

Some in the crowd join in. Maybe they know the scam, maybe they don't. Don't matter. "Leave 'em alone!" they shout. "Why you pickin' on that poor woman?"

"Where's the manager?"

Brandylin wails, "She's not, she's not, she's not a whore!"

"Look at my baby!" I shout. "Look what you done to my child." I pull Brandylin into my arms. We're way over the top, but it's hard not to stop. "I want the manager. I want to speak to—"

"What's the problem here?" Another cracker joins the group of servers. He's all frowns and concerns and turns to the Arab sayin', "Doctor, what's the problem? What's going on?"

"Mommy's no whore!"

"Hate speech!" someone shouts.

"My daughter's not a thief!"

It's a good show. Academy Award. But all good things come to an end. And when it does, when everyone settles and Brandylin's tears stop, we finally get the manager to give us a room with lots of apologies. 'Specially from Dr. Arab. Everyone says they're sorry, 'cept for Mr. Kind Eyes who jus' keeps smilin' sadly. Oh, and the Asian chick. She won't back down neither, even when the doctor dude demands it.

Then again, maybe she's got reasons. 'Cause when the manager takes us upstairs and shuts the door to our new accommodations, I pretty soon hear this jinglin' and turn to see Brandylin holdin' the bracelet.

My eyes kinda widen. "How did . . . ?"

My baby smiles. "When she put it back on the counter, durin' all the commotion, I snagged it."

I have to smile. She does got street smarts.

That night we sleep happily ever after. Well, Brandylin does. And me, mostly. But no matter what I do, I can't get them eyes out of my head. Try as I might, I jus' keep seein' 'em lookin' at me and smilin'. Not judgy or nothin'. Just like they know me . . . and like me anyways.

eighteen

B
E
R
N
A
R
D

It was kinda like a campfire, but without all that bother-some smoke or fire or camping stuff. But we did have popcorn. Tuesday night is always popcorn night. So we were all eating popcorn and writing out our lists for Trashman and talking about the day's excitement with Jamal and the soup kitchen and everything.

Of course, my list was a little longer than normal thanks to calling that homeless lady names, 'cept I actually don't remember saying everything she said I said, although I do remember what her robe told me about her being royalty and all.

Of course, on the way home, Dr. Aadil had been pretty worked up and he gave us all a good talking to about manners and respect and everything. Max tried to explain that it was all a misunderstanding, but Dr. Aadil cut him off. Not real mean, but you didn't have to be a peace monitor to tell he thought Max was one of the ones responsible.

Anyway, I was a little sad not seeing Chloe there, in the TV room, I mean. She'd been staying in her room a lot more in the evenings and it bothered me. Not bothered, more like it made me a little sad. Funny, me and her barely talk, but when she's around I always feel better. When I asked Darcy, she said Chloe had another one of her headaches, but Darcy's dragons were already shaking their heads like it wasn't true.

"You believe that, Crazy Boy, then you're more stupid than you look," One Eye said.

"That ain't possible," his partner said, sucking a cigarette and blowing out the smoke. "No one can be that stupid."

"Then what is he?"

"Just crazy." He looked up to me. "Ain't that right, Crazy Boy. You're just crazy."

I didn't bother to answer. I just figured Chloe was upset because she accused that lady's daughter of being a thief when she wasn't. As usual, Max tried to make her feel better. He said something about me and Chloe seeing stuff that's got more truth in it than just being true. I nodded like I knew what he was talking about, which I didn't, but sometimes you just got to do that to make him feel better.

Anyways, when Trashman showed up in the TV room, we all tossed our lists in his bag except for Darcy, and Chloe, who wasn't there, and of course, Jamal. I'd been thinking a lot about Jamal. I bet we all were. They say Sacramento is the best place for getting well if you're really sick. But why we never get postcards from friends who go there is beyond me. Actually, it isn't beyond me. I just try not to think about it.

Eventually it was time for bed and we all shuffled past Nurse Hardgrove's station to get our medication, then past Darcy's station to give it up, then to our rooms. After brushing and flossing, I said goodnight to my nightlight and to Max. Then I climbed into bed, and went to sleep.

The dream started right where it left off the night before—on top of that hill, me and Max dancing to Trashman's music. But we were only going a little while before Trashman had this idea. He stopped playing and pointed down the hill to the grassy meadow below us.

"What's up?" Max asked.

He pointed to the hill again. Then he made motions like we should all get on our hands and knees and roll down it.

Max laughed. "You're not serious?"

He nodded and went through the motions again.

"You want us to roll down the hill?"

"Sí." Trashman grinned. "Sí."

Max turned to me. I didn't know what he was going to do until he broke into that smile of his.

"Oh, no," I said. "Really?"

"Sure. Why not?"

I could think of a hundred reasons why not, but at the moment none came to my mind.

"Come on, let's do it!" Max lowered himself to the ground, groaning a little, until he stretched himself out on the edge of the hill.

I just stood there watching.

"Well, come on, guys." He motioned for us to join him

Trashman kinda giggled like he didn't expect Max to actually do it. I kinda prayed like I hoped he wouldn't.

But Max was already on the ground, so Trashman got down and joined him. That left yours truly.

"Come on, Bernie." Max said.

"You're really going to do this?"

They both nodded.

I looked over my shoulder, down to my little monument of rocks. Then past them to the nice foggy forest. What had I gotten myself into?

"Bernie."

"Okay, okay." I got onto my hands and knees. Then, after giving the guys one last look, I stretched out onto the grass beside them.

"Everyone set?" Max asked.

Trashman giggled. "Sí."

"Sure," I mumbled.

Suddenly, without warning, Trashman pushed off. He'd barely started before he began whooping and hollering, all the time rolling faster and faster.

"Wait up!" Max shouted.

"Max, are you really—"

He pushed off . . . doing his own brand of whooping and hollering.

So now it was just me. I scooted up closer to the edge. I rocked forward, then stopped. Then started, then stopped. I guess the third time is the charm because that's when I went over the edge and gravity took over. The hill was pretty steep, so I really picked up speed. The others were rolling ahead of me, yelling and laughing. I kept rolling and yelling too, though I wasn't so sure about the laughing. I mean I was going so fast I couldn't stop even if I wanted to. That was scary, being out of control like that. But it was also fun. Scary and fun.

By the time I reached the bottom of the hill, I was also laughing. I tried getting to my feet but stumbled and staggered around like I was drunk. The other guys were staggering, too. And laughing. Everyone was laughing—Trashman more than the two of us combined. I got the feeling he'd been wanting to do this his whole life but couldn't find anybody to do it with until now. And now he was having the time of his life. Honestly, he was letting go with huge belly laughs so big he had to bend over just to catch his breath. And when he looked up, tears were streaming down his face.

If that wasn't enough, while we were still trying to recover, he turned and scampered back up the hill.

"What?" Max shouted. "Again?"

Still laughing, Trashman motioned for us to follow.

"All right!" Max started after him then looked back to me. "Come on!"

I nodded and followed. Who wouldn't? By the time I got to the top I was really sucking in air and wheezing, but it didn't matter. I was having too much fun.

We threw ourselves onto the grass and did it all over again. Trashman, me and Max, round and round and round, laughing and shouting and trying to breathe.

When I finally reached the bottom, everything kept spinning so much I could barely sit up. "Yes!" I yelled, trying to catch my breath through the laughing. "This . . . is . . . great!"

But the other two didn't answer.

"Guys?" I looked around. "Guys? Where are—" Then I spotted Max. Just a few feet away. He was on his back, eyes closed. But he wasn't laughing. He wasn't even moving.

"Max!" I tried to stand, but the ground was still turning so I had to crawl on my hands and knees. "Max, wake up! Max!"

Trashman suddenly appeared between us. He kneeled down and bent over Max. And even though his shoulder and hair kind of blocked my view, I still saw what I saw.

Trashman was kissing my roommate! Right on the mouth! Right there in the open!

I was so shocked, I jolted awake in bed.

I just lay there, breathing hard, staring up at the ceiling. I closed my eyes and opened them, trying to clear my head. I rolled over to check on Max. And there, in the dim light, between our two beds, stood Trashman. He was leaning over Max, just like in the dream. And he was kissing him, just like in the dream—except he had one hand over his nose more like an artificial respiration thing.

I jolted awake again.

I shook my head from side to side, making sure I was awake this time. That's when I heard Trashman's squeaky cart. I turned to look just as the door clicked shut behind him. He was gone. I clenched my eyes again and opened them again. This time I was definitely awake.

"Hey." It was Max.

I rolled over to face him.

"You okay?" he asked.

I tried to answer, but my voice wasn't working so well.

"Bernie?"

"Yeah," I finally croaked. "I'm okay." I took another breath. "What about you? Everything . . . all right?"

Even in the dim light I could see that big grin appear. "Oh, yeah." He clasped his hands behind his head and stared up at the ceiling. "I'm better than all right. A thousand times better."

nineteen

B
E
R
N
A
R
D

I'm not one of those phobia guys, really. I mean if Max and Trashman are, you know, more than friends, I'm fine with that. It's not like I'm uneducated or anything. Besides, they were just dreams, right? Still, it was kind of a shock. And, for whatever reason, I couldn't quite get it out of my head and go back to sleep. Well, maybe I slept a little. I must have, because I woke up again. And again it was to the sound of our door closing.

I stopped breathing. Finally I whispered, "Max?"

He didn't answer.

I turned to check on him. He was sound asleep under the covers. "Hey, Max?"

Still nothing.

Something wasn't right. I looked at my radio alarm. It glowed a bright, blue 4:54 AM. I glanced up to the video camera. Its little light glowed a bright red. Even though we were supposed to stay in bed until seven, I had to get up and check on him. I mean we were still friends, right? I carefully pulled back my covers and snuck over to his bed. I didn't exactly want to touch him—not because I had hate speech thoughts or anything, but because I didn't want to, you know, send him the wrong message.

Still, something wasn't right. So I carefully reached out and touched him. "Max?" He felt weird. I shook him. "Hey, Max."

That's when I realized he wasn't there. It was just his pillow stuffed under his blankets. I looked over to the bathroom. The door was open and, except for the nightlight, everything was dark.

Great. Where'd he go?

I crept back over to my bed, thought a moment, then slipped into my furry-bear slippers. I went to my closet and put on my robe. Like I said, no one was supposed to be up this early, let alone be out of their room. But like I also said, Max was my friend and he sure didn't need anything like this on his permanent record.

I cracked open our door to look. And I gasped. It was worse than I thought. Three doors down, Nelson had stepped out of his room and the two of them were walking down the hallway. I quickly shut the door and leaned against it. What was he doing? I closed my eyes and thought. He was new. Maybe he'd forgotten. Someone should warn him. As a friend, wasn't it my responsibility to—

No. Everyone knows the rules and everyone follows them—well, except Jamal and look what happened to him. My record was perfect. After all these years it was still as neat as a pin, and that's how I was going to keep it.

Except Max was my friend. He was—

No. Absolutely not.

I glanced up to the security camera. Even now, if they saw what I was doing, I'd be in trouble. But I could fix that. I'd just pretend I had to go to the bathroom. Still, even as I crossed to it, my mind raced. What was Max thinking? Was he crazy? Well of course he was crazy. But shouldn't somebody tell him?

I entered the bathroom and snapped on the switch.

"Argh! Stow the light, lad!" I looked down to the pirate nightlight. "You want ta be blindin' us all?"

"Sorry." I turned off the switch.

He grunted in reply.

"Sorry," I repeated. (Inanimate objects appreciate politeness.)

"So tell me it ain't true. Are ye really desertin' yer mate like some rat on a sinkin' ship."

"I'm not deserting him."

"'Ye ain't offerin' him no hand."

"He knows the rules. If he wants to leave, he—"

"Bilge water."

Another voice from inside the medicine cabinet spoke up. "What's the matter, you?" Against my better judgment, I opened the door to see my electric razor. The one my old roommate had brought from Italy. "You said he was your friend."

"Well, he is . . . he was . . . but—"

"Friends, they don't behave that way."

"Aye," the nightlight agreed. "Once a mate, always a mate."

"He's still my friend," I said. "He's still my mate."

"Then what ye be doin' standin' here, lad. Get out thar and throw him a line."

I stood a long moment thinking. They waited a longer moment waiting. (Inanimate objects can really be persuasive). Finally, I began to nod.

"Alrightee lad," the nightlight exclaimed. "Time to be a hero."

The shaver applauded—or whatever electrical appliances do when they're excited—and I turned and headed out of the bathroom.

"Go get 'em lad."

I paused at the door, then opened it. I took a deep breath and then another before stepping into the hall-way. Forget the video cameras. Forget the permanent record. That was my friend out there and I was going to save him.

I headed down the hall, its lights dimmed for the night. I passed Nurse Hardgrove's station, which was now deserted, and entered the TV room. And there he was, sitting side by side with Nelson. But instead of making out or anything like that, they were at a table studying a piece of paper. I wasn't sure what to do so I cleared my throat.

Max looked up and grinned. "Hey, Bernie."

"Hi," I said.

"You're up early."

"Yeah. I couldn't sleep. I had this real weird dream and when I woke up I saw, well, I saw . . ." The sentence kind of faded.

Max just smiled his smile.

"So . . ." I shoved my hands into the pockets of my robe, trying to look nonchalant. "What are you guys doing?"

"That's a good question," Max said. "Nelson, here, has agreed to help me with some research." He chuckled. "The man's a walking library."

Without looking up Nelson quoted, "An investment in knowledge pays the best interest."[14]

Max motioned to the paper. "We're trying to figure something out. Come see."

Grateful for the invitation, I crossed over and joined them. On the table was a piece of paper with a bunch of handwriting on it. The first line read:

He breathed on them and said to them, "Receive the Holy Spirit."[15]

I frowned and looked up to Max. "Holy Spirit? What's that?"

"I'm not sure."

I looked back down. "And who's the, 'he'?"

Max shook his head. He leaned back in his chair and pushed up his glasses. "All I know is that God told me I won't be visiting Him anymore."

"What? Why? We like it when you visit. You always come back with neat stuff."

He nodded. "I like it, too. But He said it's no longer necessary. He said . . ." Max paused a second, then continued. "He said He's living inside me now."

"Inside you? God? Max, I don't want to be rude, but that's crazy."

He grinned. "You think?" He leaned forward and pointed at another line. "Check this out."

I looked down and read:

Do you not know that you are the temple of God and that the Spirit of God lives in you?[16]

Now I was really confused. But to be honest, I was still pretty bothered about him not getting to visit God anymore. "So God's not going to tell you what to do, or any more cool stuff?"

Max shook his head. "I didn't say that." He motioned back to the paper and I read another line:

> I will put My Spirit <u>within you</u> and cause you
> to walk in My Statutes . . .[17]

I scrunched my face into a frown.
"And check this out." He pointed to another line.

> We know that <u>we live in Him and He in us,</u>
> because He has given us His Spirit.[18]

"That makes no sense," I said. "If God's supposed
to live inside you, how are you supposed to live inside
Him?"
He nodded.
"So, which is it?"
"I have no idea. Here's another."
I looked down and read:

> <u>I am in My Father,</u> and <u>you are in Me,</u> and <u>I
> am in you.</u>[19]

And another:

> Remain <u>in Me,</u> and I will remain <u>in you.</u>[20]

"Max . . ." I closed my eyes, trying to make it make sense—which, as you've probably guessed by now, I'm not always so good at. But I didn't have long, because the doors to the main lobby suddenly flew open and the lights came up full. Two guys ran in. I'm guessing they were Security by the way they were dressed and the way they shouted. "Go to your rooms! Go to your rooms, now!"

They might have been overacting a little. I mean getting up early and meeting together was wrong, but—

"What's going on?" Max asked.

They ran right past us and toward the hallway. "Go to your rooms!"

Me, Max and Nelson looked at each other. You didn't have to be a genius to know something was up, so we rose and followed them. By the time we got to the hallway they were just going inside Chloe's and Darcy's room. My heart sank. Were they getting busted too?

Darcy stepped out. She looked as white as a sheet.

"What's wrong?" I called.

She didn't answer.

"Darcy?" Max said. "Are you okay?"

For the first time I could remember she didn't have a clever putdown. And when we got there, she just looked at us. It was like she saw us, but not really.

"Darcy?" Max put his hand on her shoulder. "What's wrong?"

Her voice was raspy, barely above a whisper. "Chloe's . . . dead."

twenty

D
R

A
A
D
I
L

It was just past 6:00 AM when Dr. Hague called. I'd already been up a good hour. Despite the nightly doses of Serotonin, which barely rate as placebos, there were those multiple, low-yield excursions to the bathroom. Old age has its privileges, I just haven't discovered them yet.

"Who found her?" I asked, slipping on my overcoat and taking the seven and half steps from my bed to the front door. Government salary also has its privileges.

"Darcy Hamilton."

"Her roommate?"

"Yes."

I would have asked why someone in Security had not spotted this on the videos they're so fond of, but now was not the time. I unbolted the locks on my door. "And the rest of the pod?"

"Everyone is up and watching. I considered lockdown, but given the situation I thought it best—"

"No, you're right. They're a tight-knit group. They need each other's support."

"How soon before you arrive?"

I closed the door behind me and began locking its locks. "Give me twenty minutes."

He gave me fifteen. I'd just pulled up to the gate. The red and yellow lights from an EMS vehicle at the loading dock flashed across the faces of a small, huddled group. My phone chirped and I answered, "Aadil, here."

Hague replied, "They found a note."

"Just now?" I nodded to the guard who buzzed open the gate.

"The roommate was hiding it. Ms. Wong had been having sex with one of our daytime attendants."

The crowd at the dock looked over and watched as I pulled up and parked. "Voluntarily?"

"Yes and no. She was doing it for extra meds."

I turned off the ignition. "That's impossible. Chloe has been fighting me about taking her medication for weeks."

Raphael, Joseph, Nelson, and Winona approached. There was no missing their looks of grief and fear.

"Not for herself." Hague said.

"Then who?"

Winona called to me, "Dr. Aadil."

"Hang on . . ." I spoke into the phone as I opened the car door and climbed out.

"Did you hear of the tragedy?" Raphael was in tears. It was one of the few times I'd seen him without his cape and shower cap. "I am holding myself personally responsible."

I shook my head. "It's not your fault." I spoke back into the phone, "Who?"

"Her roommate. Darcy Hamilton had been forcing Chloe to prostitute herself for drugs, which she sold through outside connections."

"Dr. Aadil?" Joseph's voice was clogged with emotion. "What should we do?"

Raphael wiped his eyes. "What course of action do you recommend?"

"Everybody, back inside," I said. "Let's go back up to the pod."

"But, how shall we pursue the—"

"We'll discuss that later. For now, everyone inside."

They turned and we headed for the loading dock. Hague wasn't quite finished.

"There's something else you need to know."

"What's that?"

He hesitated before answering. "She killed herself because of Maxwell Portenelli."

I slowed to a stop. "What?"

"She said he made her feel terrible."

"He's never spoken a harsh word to anyone in the group."

"'Unbelievably guilty,' she wrote. 'He makes me feel unbelievably guilty.'"

"And that's why she took her life?"

"She said it was the only way to stop the pain."

I turned to the frightened faces and resumed walking toward them, a knot of anger filling my throat. Was it possible? Had I been duped? Was it as Middleton suggested, that all the talk of love and acceptance only served as a baited hook? To catch the naïve? To entice and reel them in?

"We're having an emergency meeting at 11:00 AM."

"And the topic?" As if I didn't already know.

"11:00 AM, Doctor." The line went dead.

"Was it my fault?" Winona asked hoarsely. "Did she do it because I lost my bracelet?"

"No, I'm sure it wasn't." I slipped the phone into my pocket as we continued toward the loading dock and the flashing EMS vehicle.

"But, if I had maintained better vigilance," Raphael said.

"She seemed like such a nice girl." Joseph shook his head. "I'd never guessed her to be the type." There was sadness in his voice, but there was also a clear attitude of judgment.

"Where's Maxwell?" I asked. "Bernard?"

"Up there." Raphael motioned to the dock where the two men stood, side by side, waiting and watching.

My jaw clenched. This was it. Religion at its purest. Smug victors standing above and judging, reeking in self-righteous and holier-than-thou pride. And below, their guilt-ridden victims, suffering under the weight of condemnation, hating themselves because of their weakness. My heart hammered in my ears as we started up the steps.

Joseph called up to them, "Max, Bernie. We're going inside."

"Hello, Dr. Aadil," Bernard said.

I ignored him. And with as much self-control as possible, calmly repeated myself, "Everyone inside. Let's go back to the pod."

I avoided Maxwell's gaze as he and Bernard turned to follow. We'd barely entered through the double doors before the freight elevator arrived and rattled opened in front of us. Two paramedics emerged pushing a gurney. On it was the covered body of Chloe Wong.

I muttered in disgust at the timing. But there was nothing to be done except stop and watch in silence as they wheeled her past us toward the doors. Winona and Joseph silently wept. Raphael sobbed openly.

And Maxwell? To everyone's surprise, he stepped in front of the gurney and put up his hands, motioning for it to stop.

Startled, the paramedics complied.

"Max?" Some kid from night security approached. "What are you doing?"

"Maxwell," I said.

But he paid no attention to either of us. He simply stared down at the covered body.

"Come on, Max." The kid took his arm, but Maxwell shook it off and continued staring. Then, without a word, he reached for the blanket covering her face and pulled it back. A hush fell over the group. Once again the kid reached for him. This time Maxwell held out his hand, fingers raised, speaking in a hoarse whisper, "Please."

For whatever reason, the kid hesitated. Then, to our astonishment, Maxwell opened Chloe's mouth, leaned over her corpse, and put his mouth directly over hers. Some gasped. Others turned their heads in disgust.

"All right, that's enough." The kid grabbed his shoulder, but Bernard suddenly stepped in and wrapped his meaty hand around the boy's arm. "Leave him be," was all he said.

Meanwhile, Maxwell had pinched Chloe's nostrils shut with his free hand and, mouth still over hers, blew into her lungs. It was an obscene attempt at CPR. The girl had been dead nearly two hours. Before he could repeat the process, one of the paramedics joined the security kid and pulled him away.

"Let go!" Bernard tried to stop them, and a brief scuffle broke out . . . until Chloe's body convulsed then coughed.

Everyone froze and turned to watch.

She coughed again and opened her eyes. They did not stare lifelessly but seemed to focus on the fluorescents above her. We watched, speechless, as she coughed a third time and, with some effort, raised her head to look around.

Gasps and "Oh my gods" rippled through the group.

"It's . . . a miracle," Joseph whispered.

I felt a chill sweep across my shoulders.

"This is not possible," Winona said.

But it was possible. And as Chloe continued to look, the realization flooded over us like a tsunami.

"He brought her back to life!" The security kid said in awe.

Raphael spoke louder. "He raised her from the dead!"

The murmurs grew louder. Bernard giggled then laughed. Someone clapped. Another slapped the grinning miracle worker on the back.

I was as stunned as the rest. But even as I stood watching, half hoping it to be an elaborate post-mortem contraction, another fact dawned and firmly took hold. If there had been any doubt before, it was absolutely clear now. For the good of the pod, for the good of the hospital, it was important Maxwell Portenelli be transferred from our facility. And the sooner, the better.

twenty-one

B
E
R
N
A
R
N
D

As you probably guessed by now, they cancelled Circle. All the doctors were having a big pow-wow upstairs. And the rest of us were way too excited. Most of all, me. Well, I suppose Chloe had a right to be excited, too. Of course, so did Max and everybody else in the pod. To be honest, I still don't know why I grabbed the night security guy's arm. It's just, and I know this is weird, but his voice sounded exactly like one of those boulders pinning me down in my dreams. Course I tried to apologize to him (the guard, not the boulder) but he said he was glad I did it. Which, if I counted everybody's vote, pretty much made it unanimous.

Even though Dr. Aadil cancelled Circle, it didn't stop us from getting together. There was way too much to talk about. Of course, Darcy was in Contemplative Lockup and they still had Chloe upstairs in the infirmary, which seemed kinda silly—what are they going to do, cure her from coming back to life? But me, Ralphy, Winona, Joey, Nelson, and Max, we were all meeting. Not in the TV room since there were way too many curious folks— mostly staff from other pods who found an excuse to drop by and say hi, or stare, or introduce themselves and say hi and stare—so we moved it to me and Max's room, which was perfectly legal, though way too crowded.

"You've got to tell me what it was like," Joey kept asking. The kid was so excited he forgot to hang on to his chair. "What did you feel?"

Max shook his head. "Actually, not much. It's just . . . inside, I felt this fire, this . . . well, there's no other word for it but . . . love. There was this burning passion inside of me that had to get out."

"And help her," Ralphy said.

I nodded in excitement. "Just like I saw in my dream."

No one paid me much attention, except Max who looked over and smiled like he knew what I was talking about. Maybe he did.

"And this sensation," Winona said, "this fire? In which sector of your body was it located? Your lungs?"

He shook his head. "Deeper."

"Ah, the passion of the heart," Ralphy said.

"No."

"Your mind?" Joey asked. "Was it something you were thinking?"

Again, he shook his head. He thought a moment, then said, "Bernie, will you hand me that tablet and pen on my desk?"

I scooped them up and passed them to him. He thought another moment, then he drew a big circle a little to the left side of the page. Inside and at the top left of it, he wrote the word, HEART.

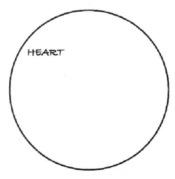

"It's as if this is my heart," he said. "All of my emotions, all my feelings."

I leaned in for a better look.

He continued, "But they're not always right, are they? We can't always trust our emotions."

"Affirmative," Winona said. "Feelings interfere with the intellectual process. It is the strength of the mind that marks a superiorly evolved race."

"Really?" he said. "Is that really true?"

Before she answered, he drew another circle on the right half of the page. Near the top, he wrote the word, MIND. But like the HEART circle, it was too big to stay on its side of the paper, so the two circles overlapped in the middle.

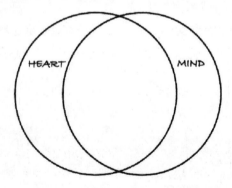

"Is the mind always right?" he asked. "Aren't we constantly replacing outdated facts with newer and more accurate ones?"

"He's got a point," Joey said.

"Like the earth may actually be round?" Winona shot back.

Joey shook his head, subtly taking hold of his chair. "Unsubstantiated rumors."

"We have pictures."

"Photoshop."

Max ignored them and pointed to the smaller space where the two circles overlapped. "And this section here, what would you call it?"

We stared at the picture real hard, but no one had an answer.

"Isn't this who we really are?" Max said. "We're not simply heart, and we're not simply mind, but aren't we a combination of both?"

"In my country, one would call such a thing the soul," Ralphy said. "It is the soul that makes up the true man."

Max nodded. "That's right, we talked about that." He wrote out the word, SOUL in the smaller space.

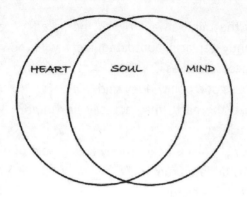

Nelson began bobbing. "' Love the Lord your God with all your *HEART* and with all your *SOUL* and with all your *MIND*.'"[21]

No one said anything as we all just stared at the paper.

"But I think there's one more part," Max said. "I think we're leaving something out. It's what Nelson, Bernie, and I discussed earlier this morning." He looked at me like I had the answer.

I smiled but was clueless.

He looked down and began drawing a tiny little circle inside the SOUL space and then he colored it in.

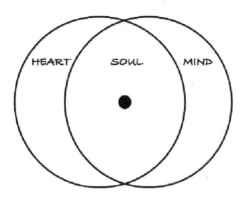

"What is that?" Joey said.

"I think . . . Now remember this is all new to me. But I think that part . . . I think it is the *SPIRIT*."

"The what?"

"The *SPIRIT* of God."

Everyone got extra quiet, well, except me, 'cause I finally remembered. "*THAT'S* what we were talking about!"

He looked up and smiled.

"Sure is puny," Joey said, "compared to the other parts, I mean."

"At first, yes. But, like anything else, if I feed it, it grows."

"What do you mean," Winona said. "How do you feed it?"

"It's like we said earlier, by remaining in God's presence. By feeding upon *HIM*."

Nelson bobbed. "'The one who feeds on Me will live because of Me.'"[22]

There was more silence.

Finally Joey asked, "This Spirit you're talking about. Is that what you breathed into Chloe?"

"Yes. It was the fire I felt inside of me, the love I had to share."

We were all too surprised to speak.

"And there's more." Max started getting even more excited. "As I feed upon him, as his Spirit grows inside of me, it starts influencing me." He drew arrows shooting out from the little circle. Then he made a bigger circle around them.

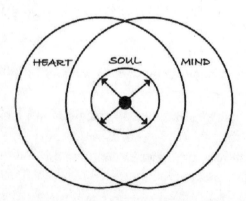

"It starts directing my heart *AND* my mind—helping me feel things the way He feels them, and to think about things the way He thinks about them. He drew the arrows even bigger, out to the very edge.

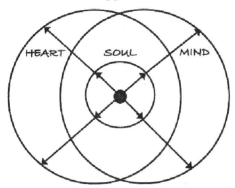

Nelson gave another quote, "You, however, are controlled not by sinful nature but by the Spirit, if the Spirit of God lives in you."[23] He paused, then added, "For it is God who works in you to will and to act according to *HIS* good purpose."[24]

Max nodded. "God . . . not me. God. I don't have to do all those good things that make people good or moral or religious. And I don't have to avoid all the bad things that make people bad."

"God does it for you," Joey said.

"Right. Goodness is still my goal. It's just how I get there. Instead of trying to do it on my own, where I'm always failing and feeling guilty, I let God do it. And the best thing is, it happens naturally . . . as naturally as a tree growing fruit."

Again Nelson quoted, "The fruit of the Spirit is love, joy, peace, patience, kindness, goodness, faithfulness, gentleness and self-control."[25]

"Hold it," Max said. "Let me write those down."

Nelson repeated, "The fruit of the Spirit is love, joy, peace—"

"A little slower."

He took a breath and quoted the words even slower as Max wrote them out at the bottom of the page.

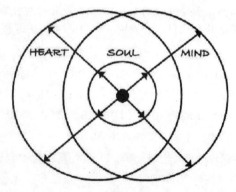

LOVE, JOY, PEACE, PATIENCE, KINDNESS, GOODNESS, FAITHFULNESS, GENTLENESS, SELF-CONTROL

We all stared at the paper.

Finally, Winona spoke, "That would be a wonderful way to live."

"But who can do it?" Joey said.

Max nodded, "Exactly. No one can. That's why they're called the fruit of the *SPIRIT*. Not the fruit of *JOEY*, not the fruit of *WINONA*, or the fruit of *MAX*. They come from His Spirit. It's God doing His work inside us. Not us doing it, but God."

Nelson fired off another quote. "If a man remains in me and I in him, he will bear much fruit."[26]

"So, all we must do is remain in him," Winona said.

Joey quoted something else. And the cool thing was, I remembered it from when we talked about it before. "Be still and know He's God."

Everyone nodded like they remembered it, too.

After a long moment, Winona finally summed it up. "It's like you've been saying . . . we just let God love us and love Him back."

Max nodded. "Like a little child and his perfect father."

Everybody got real, real still. But there was one more question and it didn't look like anyone was going to ask it. So I cleared my throat and said, "Max?"

He turned to me.

"Would you . . . you know? Would you do to me what you did to Chloe . . . what Trashman did to you?"

He broke into another one of his grins.

"And me," Winona said.

"Me, too," Ralphy added.

"And me," Joey said.

He was just getting ready to answer when Biff (or was it Britt?) poked his head into the room. "Max?" He stood in the doorway, looking all serious. "Will you come with me, please?"

"Now?" Max glanced around at us.

The orderly nodded.

"Why?" Winona asked. You could tell she sounded suspicious.

So did Joey. "What's going on?"

"Never fear," Ralphy rose to his feet. "Raphael Montoya Hernandez III is here to protect and defend."

Britt (or was it Biff?) shook his head. "There's nothing to protect and defend him from. Unless it's his daughter."

"My daughter?" Max's voice got just a little high and uneven. "She's here? She's come to visit?"

Biff (or was it Britt?) nodded. "Her and Dr. Aadil. They're waiting to meet you up in Dr. Hague's office."

I looked back to Max. You could see the color kind of draining from his face.

"Why there?" Joey asked. "Why now?"

Britt (or was it Biff?) just shrugged. But you could tell something was up. We all could.

"Don't go," Winona said.

Ralphy agreed. "I fear it is a trick."

"They just want to talk." Max said. He looked to the orderly, obviously hoping for a nod.

He didn't get it. Britt (or was it Biff?) just stepped to the side, waiting for Max to join him.

Max glanced around the table one last time and finally pushed back his chair to stand.

"Max . . ." I warned.

He patted me on the shoulder and began working his way through the crowded room. "A lot has happened," he said. "I'm sure they just want to talk."

"Be careful, Señor."

He flashed us that smile. It was supposed to make us feel better. It would have helped if it made it all the way up to his eyes.

"Max?" I called.

But he didn't look back. He just raised his hand in a little wave. Then he stepped through the doorway and disappeared into the hall.

twenty-two

A
L
E
X
I
S

"We're sedating him now," Dr. Aadil said.

"That's necessary?" I asked as we headed down the hallway.

"It's standard practice when transporting patients. It helps calm and relax them."

I wondered how I could get a hit for myself. Seriously, the doctor's call couldn't have come at a worse time. Actually, that's a lie. Any time was a good time to get away from my hovering minions with their forced praises and smiles that screamed, "Amateur! Fraud! We're going to expose you!"

The hospital was decorated in late American cliché. Everywhere I looked there were Photoshopped mountains, Photoshopped meadows and waterfalls with smeary, out-of-focus water. The walls were no better, painted so happy and cheery they'd make a Chuck E. Cheese jealous. And let's not forget my host's fashion statement: Retro Rest Home.

"Will I be able to visit him there?" I asked.

"Is that a priority?"

"Well, yeah. I mean, sure."

He nodded. "I don't recall you visiting him while he was here."

Touché.

"Their regiment and procedures are much more stringent than ours. A visit from the outside could conflict with whatever therapy they may choose for him."

We rounded the corner and I nearly gasped at the garish bulletin board of Crayon kiddie art. Even with sunglasses, it hurt the eyes. Then again . . .

I slowed and pulled out my smartphone. "Do you mind if I take a photo?"

"Hospital regulations are a bit sticky on that."

I nodded and began snapping away. "It'll only take a second. Anything's better than dental floss."

"Pardon me?

I didn't bother to answer. After a dozen quickies, I dropped the phone back into my purse and started down the hall again.

"You'd asked about visits," he said.

"Yeah. What about them?"

"If you make appropriate arrangements ahead of time, I am sure a visit would not be impossible." The old-timer was choosing his words pretty carefully.

"And you honestly think it will help?" I said. "Shipping him off like this?"

We slowed to a stop in front of a large, closed door.

"We have done everything we can."

"But it's only been a few weeks."

"The committee has carefully weighed its options and firmly believes Sacramento will be much more helpful in your father's recovery."

Before I could respond, he pushed open the door to a large room with a single row of beds. Scattered up and down were five or six patients, all dozing. And there, in the very first bed, slept my father. My throat tightened. In all my years, I'd never seen him look so frail, so . . . vulnerable.

"Mr. Portenelli?" the doctor said. "Maxwell?"

Father stirred and opened his eyes. When they focused, he spotted us, grinned and slurred out a, "Hey there, Doc."

"How are we feeling?"

"Fantastic. How are you?"

"Fine," the doctor said, "just fine."

Still smiling, Father turned to me. "Hello." There was zero recognition in his eyes and my throat tightened even more.

"You remember your daughter? Alexis?"

Father frowned then broke into another smile. "You're the young lady who brought me here."

I nodded, blinking back the emotion, grateful for my sunglasses. But he must have sensed something because his smile quickly faded. He spoke again, his voice softer, thicker. "I'm sorry." He reached out and took my hand.

I looked down, startled at the gesture.

"I'm so very sorry," he said again.

I adjusted my glasses, forcing a smile. "No problem. The doctors say it's only temporary."

He looked to the doctor and got a nod.

We stood a moment in silence.

I cleared my throat. "He tells me they're moving you to another hospital."

"Yes."

More silence. I glanced down at my hand, thinking I should remove it, but not sure how. "Supposed to make you better," I said. "Get you all fixed up so you can get back to work and crack the whip."

He nodded. "And you?"

"I'm sorry?"

"How are you?"

"Good. I'm real good."

I saw concern flicker across those glassy eyes. I cranked up my smile, but I'm pretty sure he didn't buy it.

More silence as he kept staring.

"Well," the doctor finally stepped in, "we've got some paperwork to sign. I just thought it important you two have a chance to say goodbye."

"And it's not really goodbye," I said. "I mean when you stop to think about it, Sacramento's not that far away. Only a few hours." I was jabbering like a nervous schoolgirl. "We could drive there and drop in to visit anytime. Just say the word and, well, you know . . . we . . ." I finally got control and forced myself to stop.

"So." The doctor reached for the chart at the foot of the bed. "I'd advise getting some rest. Might as well get your money's worth from that sedative." Forced chuckles all around. "We'll get things started with that paperwork and have you on the road in no time."

Father nodded and gave my hand a little pat. "We'll see you later then," he said.

"Yes, later." Gently, but with some effort, I withdrew my hand. I dredged up another smile, adjusted my glasses, and turned for the door.

"Excuse me?" he said.

I turned back.

"Fathers and daughters, don't they normally hug?"

I shot a look to the doctor, who'd busied himself with the chart. We were *NOT* a huggy family. Never were. Oh sure, there was the obligatory greeting, the brush of cheeks, it came with the work. But that's not what he had in mind, not as he lifted his arms to me. What was going on? Was it the drugs?

I stole another glance to the doctor. But he was busy, and the man in the bed continued to wait.

Well, all right. I mean if it made him feel better.

I stepped back to the bed and bent down. He wrapped both arms around me. But when I tried to rise, he pulled me in even closer until his mouth was next to my ear. Then he whispered, "You are loved. Never forget that. You are loved more than you know."

The words caught me off guard. I pulled from the hug and readjusted my glasses.

He smiled and I returned it. Then, giving him an obligatory nod, I turned, took a moment to get my bearings, and walked away—my throat so tight I could barely breathe.

twenty-three

B
E
R
N
A
R
D

It was Chinese Food Night, but I, for one, wasn't hungry. The sweet and sour whatever-it-was wasn't bad, but I just pushed the fried rice around with my fork, carefully aligning each grain to point the proper direction so my plate looked like a giant crop circle. I was hoping Winona would notice and maybe offer to let me join her on her next expedition, but like everyone else, she just sat there all quiet and glum.

Even the inanimate objects were inanimate.

Outside, in the courtyard, I could hear Trashman playing his recorder—the same breathy tune he always played. Of course I glanced around, making sure I wasn't the only one hearing it. But the way everybody seemed to listen, I figured I was in good company.

After what seemed forever, Winona finally broke the silence. "It is mandatory we divide into shifts."

"For what?" Joey said.

"In the event they attempt an evening abduc-tion."

"We've been watching all afternoon, there's been nothing."

Joey was right. We'd all been watching the parking lot since they took Max upstairs. There'd been a few visitors, but no State vans like the type they transport patients in.

"He's still here," Joey said. "Somewhere."

But somewhere was a big place, at least in our hospital. Not even Nurse Hardgrove or Biff (or was it Britt?) knew. If they did they weren't telling.

I sighed. "Even if we found him, what could we do?"

"We could avenge their crime." Ralphy adjusted his goggles. "We will throw off the yoke of oppression and free the world of their tyranny."

"Maybe we could go on a hunger strike," Joey said.

Winona looked at her uneaten food. "Perhaps we could commence now."

Ralphy said, "We must devise a plan of attack."

"Why?" Joey asked.

"I do not understand the question," Ralphy said.

"What if they're right? What if Max is just another loon?" A little more sadly, he added, "What if he's just like the rest of us."

The words hit as hard as any that had been spoken from tattoos or boulders. What if they were true? What if Max wasn't special or loved. What if none of us were? I thought back to the mural at the National Science Museum, the one with the caption, "You are barely here." It made me even sadder.

"Well, I, for one, shall never admit defeat," Ralphy said. "I shall always believe him."

Winona didn't bother to glance up. "So they can transport you to Sacramento, too?"

That's when things got quiet. *REAL* quiet.

Until Joey suddenly cried out, "Holy crud on a cracker!"

I turned to see that he'd opened his fortune cookie and was reading the fortune.

"What?" Winona said.

He passed it to her. She read it and her mouth dropped open.

"What does it say?" Ralphy asked.

She read it out loud. "You are my favorite son. God."

I couldn't believe my ears.

Joey took it back and reread it.

"Señor, Joey," Ralphy said, "does this mean that you have been chosen to replace Max?"

"Let the word go forth . . ." Nelson quoted. "The torch has been passed to a new generation."[27]

Ralphy opened his own fortune and stared down at it. "Such a thing as this, it is not possible."

"What?" I said."

He read, "You are my favorite son. God."

We paused a second then quickly grabbed our own cookies. I was the first to get mine open.

"What's it say?" Joey asked.

I read, "You are my favorite son. God."

Nelson read his. "'You are my favorite son. God.'"

We turned to Winona who was the last to open hers.

"Well?" Joey asked.

She shook her head. I felt a wave of pity. She was such a nice person. She turned it around so we could all read: "You are my favorite daughter. God."

"Me too."

I looked up to see Chloe arrive at our table. Her cookie had already been opened with the fortune lying on her tray.

"Here, let me help," I said, getting up and taking the tray.

Everyone greeted her and she tried her best to smile, which, let's face it, still wasn't her strong suit.

"It's great to see you," I said.

She nodded. "The infirmary."

"Did they run a bunch of tests on you up there?" I asked.

"Really drugged up," she said. "They're moving him early in the morning."

I frowned. "You mean they gave you *MORE* drugs?"

She looked at me like I'd said something more stupid than usual.

"Have you heard anything regarding Max?" Winona asked.

Chloe looked at her with equal frustration.

"Do you know his location?"

She scowled.

"I think she already told us," Joey said.

"The infirmary?" Winona asked. "He's in the infirmary?"

Chloe nodded like it was obvious.

"And he's drugged up so they can move him later tonight?" Joey said.

Again she nodded.

Suddenly, Ralphy leaped to his feet. "I shall not sit here and allow such evil." Flipping his bath towel to the side, he turned and immediately headed for the hallway.

"Ralphy," I called. "Where you going?"

He raised his arm high into the air and pointed forward.

I turned to the others. "Does he have a plan?"

Winona adjusted her foil sleeves and rose to her feet. "If he doesn't, we shall devise one. Let us proceed."

I turned to Joey who also started to stand, along with Chloe and Nelson . . . and me.

twenty-four

B
E
R
N
A
R
D

"You sure you can unlock this thing?" Joey asked Winona.

"Kid stuff. On my planet we learn such things in prenatal school."

Everyone watched as she took a piece of aluminum foil and worked it around the buttons of the hallway's electronic door lock. Well, everyone watched but me and Ralphy. We were busy holding his bath towel up over everyone's head.

"Please, make haste," Ralphy called. "The Invisibility Cloak does not have unlimited power."

Neither do my arms, I thought. I threw a look up to the security camera in the corner. "How exactly does this thing work?" I asked.

"You do not see?" he asked.

"Sorry," I said, "no."

"Exactly. And neither do they."

I nodded. It's hard arguing with superhero logic.

"Okay," Winona ordered, "everyone stand back."

I clenched my eyes, waiting for the explosion and heard . . .

Nothing.

"Hang on."

She tinkered some more and . . .

There was nothing some more. Except for one or two groans. And Nelson, who had been humming. The tune wasn't anything special, just the same notes over and over again.

"Will you knock it off?" Joey whispered.

He kept humming.

"Nelson!" Winona hissed.

He stopped just long enough to quote, "Music expresses that which cannot be said."[28]

"What are you talking about?" Joey said.

"Wait a minute," Winona said. "Is that the code? Have you memorized the numerical tones for the lock?"

"Of course."

She shook her head in frustration. "Okay. Give them to me again. Only slow, one note at a time."

"Please, my friends," Ralphy said, "we must hurry."

Nelson hummed the notes and Winona eventually found the right buttons to push in the right order.

"Nine, five, eight, five," Nelson asked.

"You knew all along?" Winona said. "Why didn't you tell us?"

"'Real knowledge is to know the extent of one's ignorance.'"[29]

Winona muttered, turned the knob and pushed open the door. Everyone piled through it, with me and Ralphy bringing up the rear and Ralphy yelling, "The plan! Follow the plan!"

Of course there was no plan, not really. And if there was, we were way too excited to remember. We raced down the hallway, up a flight of stairs and down another hall where Surveillance had their control room—just like Nelson remembered from the "In Case of Fire" diagram Nurse Hardgrove had in her office.

Once we arrived and everyone got in position, Winona whispered, "Okay. On my count. One—"

But Ralphy wasn't real good at math. He threw himself against the door and it flew open. "I am Raphael Montoya Hernandez III," he shouted staggering into the dimly lit room. "Step away from the video monitors and no one gets hurt."

But, of course there was no one at the video monitors, just one of the security guys asleep on a sofa at the back wall. Well, he had been asleep. Now he was busy leaping to his feet and using some of Darcy's favorite potty-mouth words.

"Stay back!" Ralphy shouted. "You have been warned!"

Me, Chloe, and Nelson joined his side as Winona and Joey raced to the control panel to shut down the video monitors on the front wall.

"Who are you guys?" The security man was still pretty groggy and trying his best to get more awake . . . and a little more sober.

Ralphy shouted, "We have come to liberate the unliberated, to up-trodden the downtrodden, to—"

Nelson interrupted, "'—proclaim freedom for the captives—'"[30]

I added, "To boldly go where no superheroes have gone before!"

They all turned to me and I kind of shrugged.

"How are you doing?" Joey called to Winona.

"I am having difficulty locating the power switch."

The security guy shook his head. "Wow, superheroes. I'm really honored."

"Thank you," I said.

"So do you have, like, guns and stuff?"

"We are superheroes," Ralphy said. "We do not need guns."

"Oh. Well, in that case." The guy reached into his black holster and pulled out a rather large looking revolver.

"Status report," Winona called to Joey.

"I've got nothing . . . except one large, red button."

"Depress it," Winona said.

He depressed it and an ear-splitting alarm began to blast . . . along with the flashing of a rather obnoxious red light.

"I don't think so," Winona shouted.

Meanwhile, the security guy waved his gun at us, motioning us back toward the sofa. "I'm not sure how you crazies got out, but get over there."

As we obeyed, I whispered to Ralphy, "Now what?"

"Plan B," he whispered back.

"Do we have a Plan B?"

"Not yet."

"Attack!" Chloe shouted over the alarm.

We turned to look at her. She slumped and pulled back into her sweater.

"I found it!" Joey yelled.

"Not so fast." The security guy spun his gun to them. "Get over here, both of you, and join—"

But never being good with following directions, Joey hit another button and all the video monitors on the wall went black. So did the light in the room. Now there was only that flashing red light and the blaring alarm which, I don't want to complain, was really starting to get on my nerves.

"Bernie?"

"Yes, Ralphy."

"Shall we attempt Chloe's plan?"

"I think she'd like that."

"I think so, too." Suddenly Ralphy screamed at the top of his lungs and ran into the darkness. I followed right behind. We managed to find the man and, although there were a few random gunshots and bunch of hitting, not to mention more bad language, we eventually got him onto the floor long enough for Nelson to use the man's shoelaces to tie him up with some very impressive-looking knots.

Once we were sure he couldn't move, and with heartfelt apologies from yours truly, we raced back into the hallway and headed down to the infirmary.

twenty-five

D
R

A
A
D
I
L

I'd certainly had better days . . . and nights. The good news was I'd finally been able to get to sleep, courtesy of a secret Navy Seals recipe involving inordinate amounts of tequila and equal parts rum. The bad news was I'd nearly twisted my sheets into a sheepshank (more Navy training), before my cell rang.

"Aadil, here," I mumbled.

"Doctor, this is Sisco Heights. Sorry to call at this late hour."

"No problem," I looked down at my knotted sheets. "I've been working on a project."

"We have a situation. It's the Portenelli transfer."

My stomach rose as my head pounded. It was not going to be a good morning. I squinted at the red blur of my radio alarm. "He's not scheduled until early morning." I squinted harder. "What time is it?"

"The patient is fine. He's sedated and in the infirmary."

"Then what—"

"It's your other patients."

I rubbed my temples. "Which ones?"

"All of them, sir."

"What!" I winced and tried again, a bit softer. "What are you saying?"

"Dr. Hague suggests you come down here."

"Is he there? Can you put him on?"

"No, sir, but—"

"What exactly is happening there?"

"Dr. Hague suggests you come to the hospital immediately. He says it's an emergency."

twenty-six

B
E
R
N
A
R
D

"Max?" I gave him a little shake. "Max, you okay?

He opened his eyes and stared up at the ceiling. I rose from beside his bed so he could see me. When he did, he broke into a goofy smile. "Hi ya, Bernie."

"Hi, Max," I whispered. "How are you feeling?"

"Just swell, Bernie. And you?"

"Oh, I'm pretty good. We missed you at dinner. It was Chinese night and I made this cool crop circle on my plate with all my—"

"That's nice . . ." He smiled, closed his eyes, and went back to sleep.

But that was okay because, thanks to Winona, we had a pretty cool plan that he really didn't need to help us with. Since Max was the first in a long line of beds in the infirmary—*DEATH ROW* they called it—me, Joey, and Nelson had snuck in and crouched down between his bed and the wall. Chloe and Ralphy were a few feet out in the hallway keeping watch, while at the other end of our room, Winona was tinkering with a bunch of monitors connected to another patient.

"Now!" Chloe whispered "Now!"

We looked to Ralphy, who shook his head. We'd pretty much learned that Chloe's "now" was a little different from the rest of our "nows." At least twenty seconds different.

A moment later, Winona called over to us. "Everyone ready?"

We peeked our heads above Max's bed and nodded.

"Okay then!" She flipped a switch and an alarm sounded—not the same as the security alarm that was still going, but it was just as irritating. Winona took off running toward us. "Get down! Get down!"

Ralphy and Chloe ducked around the corner, and we got down as Winona joined us. A moment later the doctor and a tall, skinny nurse raced in.

"He's coded!" the nurse shouted.

"Get the cart!" the doctor shouted.

This is what we in the escape business call a "Diversionary Tactic." The patient wasn't really dying. Winona had just fixed his monitor to look like he was. The idea was to get the staff so involved in saving him, that they wouldn't notice us standing up and casually rolling Max's bed out of the room. And that's exactly what happened, except for the part about not getting noticed.

As soon as the nurse rolled the cart to the patient, we got up and started pushing Max's bed—which was about the same time the doctor looked up and spotted us.

"You there! Stop!" But he was a little preoccupied, what with turning on the crash cart, jelling the paddles, and trying to save his patient's life.

"Hold it," Joey whispered as he appeared from the hallway. "If there's nothing wrong with that patient and they juice him, it could do serious damage."

"Not to worry," Winona said.

"Why's that?"

"Clear!" the doctor shouted.

"I rewired it," she said.

The machine zapped and the doctor dropped unconscious to the floor.

We turned to Winona, who shrugged. "I was a little rushed."

We started down the hallway toward the elevator when I heard some voices shouting from inside the janitor's supply closet. "In here! Don't forget us! We want to go, too!"

I glanced to my friends, but it looked like nobody heard.

"Please! Save us! Take us with you!"

Since it was right on the way, and since I'm such a pushover, I raced to the door, opened it, and snapped on the light. Sure enough, there was a whole bunch of cleaning supplies shouting, "Me! Take me! No, take me!"

"Bernie?" Joey called. "Come on!"

"Don't leave me here! I hate the dark! It gives me nightmares!"

"What if I leave the light on?" I said.

But they just kept begging. "Take me! No, take me! No, please, take me!"

Since they all seemed nice enough, and since I hate causing hurt feelings, I started scooping up the containers. Unfortunately, there were way too many, and pretty soon I only had room for a couple more. That's when the big container of blue, toilet bowl cleaner on the bottom shelf shouted, "Remember your painting!"

I looked down at him. "What?"

"The ovals. Remember, you couldn't paint circles, only ovals?"

"Bernie!" Winona yelled.

"I don't understand."

"My shape. Look at my shape. I ain't round or square like the others. I'm oval, just like you painted."

"Is that what it meant?" I said.

"Of course. It was a sign. It's me, I'm the chosen."

He seemed pretty sure, so I reached down and grabbed him. Of course, the others shouted and complained, but like I said, my arms were full, so there was nothing I could do about it. As I backed out of the closet, the containers I'd saved began thanking me. The little bottle of Windex even began weeping, "You are my hero." And the blue jug? Not a word—well except for asking me to open his cap a little because all the shaking around was giving him gas.

When I rejoined the group they were at the elevator and Ralphy was hitting the down button over and over again.

"They cut the power," Winona said.

Nelson quoted, "The best laid plans of mice and—"[31]

"The stairs!" Joey shouted.

"Or the window," my toilet bowl cleaner yelled.

"It's a three-story drop," the Windex bottle argued.

Winona and the others agreed with Joey, so they began helping Max out of the bed.

"Okay," Joey said, "just slide your legs over the edge."

I called over, "How you feeling, Max?"

He looked up to me and started to grin. But then he suddenly stopped and frowned.

"What's wrong?" I asked.

"Darcy," he said.

"What?"

He cleared his throat. "We must rescue Darcy."

Everyone kind of looked at each other.

"Sorry, Max," Winona said. "That's not our mission."

"Trust me." The look in his eyes said he meant business. "We must rescue Darcy."

twenty-seven

B
E
R
N
A
R
D

"I'm not exactly sure when it dawned on us that if Max escaped, we all had to escape. Maybe it was when we opened the door from the stairwell onto our floor and saw the two metro policemen waiting for us—one tapping his billy club, the other fingering his Taser like it had been a long time since he'd gotten to play with it. It was about then we figured that unless they changed the rules about breaking out of our pod, shutting down hospital surveillance, tying up hospital surveillance, and stealing patients out of the infirmary (while mildly electrocuting one or two medical personnel along the way), there was a good chance we'd all receive a one-way trip to Sacramento.

Anyways, as someone who never shirked his responsibility as a superhero, Ralphy boldly stepped forward to meet them. "Greetings, fellow compatriots. Raphael Montoya Hernandez III at your service."

The two officers looked at each other then back at him. The billy club tapper nodded to Joey and Winona, who were holding Max. "Put down the crazy man and walk away with your hands up."

"I am terribly sorry," Ralphy said. "Perhaps you misunderstand. We are all on the same side—fighting for truth, justice and—"

"And what you fail to understand, Taco Breath, is that we are authorized to use force."

Everyone gasped at the hate speech, except Nelson who stepped forward and recited, "California Statute 55393.2 forbids any form of malice and/or slanderous speech—"

"Put a sock in it," Taser Man ordered.

"—toward any and all animals, human or otherwise, whose feelings may be—"[32]

The billy club tapper swung his weapon against the side of Nelson's head. None of us saw it coming, especially Nelson, which explains why he dropped to the floor in a semi-unconscious heap.

"How are those feelings now?" The man sneered.

As you probably guessed, Nelson didn't have much to say about the matter. But Joey did. Suddenly, he began staggering around like he was drunk or trying to keep his balance or both.

"Whoa . . . waaa . . . wee."

"Joey," Winona shouted, "what's wrong?"

"Summer Solstice!" he cried.

"You're kidding."

"No."

"Now?"

"Now!"

What I'm about to say you can believe or not. But suddenly, Joey flew up off the floor. That's right. With the earth changing its tilt, he shot off the ground and sailed through the air toward the men. It was the weirdest thing I'd ever seen.

They must have thought so too, which explains why they weren't ready when he smashed into them causing the billy club tapper to stagger backward and hit his head on the cinderblock wall and join Nelson in the growing pile of unconsciousness on the floor.

Being the non-violent type, I ran over to help Nelson and the billy club tapper. Unfortunately, I forgot about the bottles I'd saved from the janitor's closet. Which means I forgot to set them down, which means they sort of dropped from my arms and fell to the ground. It wasn't a major problem, except when that loose cap of the blue toilet bowl cleaner popped off and spilled a little stream onto the floor. Even that wouldn't have been a problem if it wasn't for Taser Man Tasering Joey and the electricity accidentally igniting the pretty blue liquid into a pretty big flame, which followed the stream into the jug, which exploded into a pretty big ball of flame.

Well, not so much a big ball. More like a big wall.

For the most part we were on one side of the wall and the law enforcement officers were on the other. Still, we had to pick up Joey and Nelson and drag them along with Max down the hall to Contemplative Lockup where Darcy was. Taser Man would have probably gone after us, if he wasn't so busy pulling his partner to safety. And a good thing, too. Cause the other janitor supplies were screaming and shouting for their lives as their bottles melted and they mixed with each other, which would explain the deafening explosions and the *WOOSH* of even more fire.

When we arrived and got Darcy out, she looked down the hall at the flames, which were coming pretty fast. "What did you guys do?" she shouted.

I dropped my head. "It's a long, sad story."

"Quickly!" Winona shouted. "We must depart!"

twenty-eight

S
A
F
F
R
O
N

"Come on girl . . . move!"

"Been a long time since I climbed this hill," I yell. "And it weren't steep like it is now."

A fire truck goes screamin' past, followed by another.

I half wheeze, half shout, "We got plenty a time."

But JJ, he ain't in no mood for conversation. He's still pretty mad for me makin' Brandylin stay at camp. She is, too. But I'm still the Momma and I still got responsibilities. Course that didn't stop either of them from fussin'.

"Big fire like that, big buildin' like that, there be plenty to loot!" JJ had yelled. "We need all the hands we can get."

And it don't stop Brandylin from whinin' and carryin' on, neither.

But my no is no. Too dangerous. Too risky gettin' caught. And since Brandylin ain't goin' and since she ain't stayin' in camp by herself this time a night, that means Mariposa ain't goin' either. So, yeah, I guess JJ's gots plenty of reason to be mad.

We got 'bout a block to go, but it feels like a mile. Like a hundred miles. The building, some happy farm, is burnin' so bright it lights up the whole sky. I'm bettin' everyone in the city can see it.

More cops and ambulances scream past and we kinda turn our heads. Not that they can arrest us . . . yet. But they know we ain't goin' up to see the sights.

Over the noise and the poundin' of my heart, I hear music. Like someone playin' a flute but all faint and airy. I look around, thinkin' it's comin' from one of the houses. But it ain't comin' from no house . . . It's comin' from above, from the top of the hill.

"JJ! You hear that?"

Again, he don't answer.

"JJ!"

He swears and turns back to me. "What?"

"You hear that?"

He frowns. "I don't hear nothin' but them sirens and me coughin' my lungs out."

"The music, you don't hear that music?"

He shakes his head. "You crazy woman," and turns back to keep climbin' the hill.

I follow behind him thinkin' he just might be right, cause I'm still hearin' it.

I shake my head and close my eyes. But it's still there. No matter what I do, I can't get it out of my head.

twenty-nine

B
E
R
N
A
R
D

I was feeling pretty bad about burning down the hospital. And, of course, I hoped someone would rescue my salt and pepper shakers along with my nightlight and electric razor because at the moment we were kind of busy running for our lives. By now the fire was pretty much everywhere, but mostly at our heels and closing in fast.

With all the smoke, not to mention collapsing walls and ceilings, Nelson was having a harder time figuring out where we were and more importantly how to get out of wherever that was. After taking several scenic routes, we rounded a corner and, through the thick haze, saw the glass doors leading to the lobby and parking lot. The only trouble was those glass doors were filled with the flashing lights of police cars and fire trucks. Not that all the orange, red, and yellow wasn't pretty, but for the time being we were kind of nervous about visiting with any more law enforcement officers.

Then I heard it. Over the alarm. The faint, breathy music of Trashman's recorder. It came from the closed door to my right. I looked to the others, making sure it wasn't just my imagination, but they were too busy being hysterical or coughing from the smoke or, in Chloe's case, shouting, "Erasing our records!"

Even though his music hadn't gotten any better, and there was still that whole kissing Max thing that I think I got, but still wasn't so sure about, I figured I should at least poke my head in and say goodbye. So while everybody else was panicking and wondering if the food in Sacramento would be better than here, I was busy reaching for the door, pushing it open and seeing—

"Trashman!" Darcy spotted him over my shoulder.

He was sitting at a computer, behind a tiny little desk in a tiny little room, playing that airy little song. He stopped just long enough to motion us inside. We kind of looked at each other. But with the fire behind us and the police in front, we figured a visit might not hurt. The room had plenty of smoke in it, but it wasn't nearly as bad as the hallway.

As we entered, Winona shouted, "What are you doing?"

He nodded to the computer screen. As she moved around to take a look, he stood up, shoved the recorder in his back pocket, and motioned for Joey to shut the door.

Scanning the screen, Winona said, "He's brought forth all our records. Joseph Laune, Chloe Wong, Raphael Hernandez—"

"The third," Ralphy added.

"All of us," she said.

As she spoke, Trashman reached past her and hit a single key.

Her eyes widened. "He is . . . vaporizing them! He's deleting our records." She leaned forward and continued to watch. "*ALL* of them."

We moved around the desk to take a look. She was right. All sorts of information was zooming by on the screen and each time one of our names showed up it automatically disappeared.

Meanwhile, Trashman had moved to the row of filing cabinets on the opposite wall. I barely noticed as he opened a drawer and pulled out a file folder. But I did notice when he dumped the papers in the folder all over the floor.

Please understand I'm not one of those neataphobic types, but it seemed kind of rude, making a mess like that, so I stepped around the desk and asked, "What are you doing?" He didn't say anything, so I began picking up the papers.

Winona glanced from the computer. "To what subject do they pertain?"

I looked at a heading and read: "Maxwell Portenelli—Psychological Evaluation."

"He's crazy," Darcy said. "They need a file to tell us that?"

"More records?" Joey said.

Winona agreed. "Hard copy."

Trashman motioned for them to come join us.

"You want us to help you destroy those records, too?" Darcy asked.

He nodded, motioning. "Sí, Sí!"

They eased Max into the chair and joined us at the filing cabinets.

"Look for the drawer with the letter of your last name," Joey said.

I found my drawer and pulled it open. It didn't take long to spot my file because it was the thickest. I guess when you call a place home for as long as me, there's lots of memories.

"Looks like they wrote a book on you," Darcy said, as I pulled the file out.

"Yeah." I tried not to sound too proud. Then, before I even opened the cover, Trashman grabbed it from my hands—

"Hey!"

—and threw it high into the smoke-filled air. The papers flew out and fluttered to the floor.

"That's not very polite."

Everyone was so busy with their own files that they barely noticed.

Darcy read hers: "A technophobe with unhealthy interests in Wicca and other pagan forms of worship."

Winona scowled at her own. "For this they employ the services of medical personnel?"

Ralphy read: "Grandiose delusions stemming from abnormal low, self—"

Trashman grabbed the file out of his hands and, just like mine, threw it into the air so the papers scattered all over the ground.

"Excuse me!" Ralphy cried.

Trashman didn't answer but clapped his hands motioning for the rest of the group to do the same. "Así!" he shouted. "Así!"

Everyone kind of looked at each other.

"Well . . . all right." Joey shrugged and threw his papers high into the air.

Trashman clapped. "Sí, sí! Perfecto!"

Winona, Chloe, and Nelson traded looks, then did the same. Soon the air was full of flying papers. Some of us even picked up what was on the floor and threw them again. It was like one of those old-fashioned ticker tape parades you see on TV, and it was fun. Real fun. Unfortunately, the party didn't last long.

"Hey, guys," Joey pointed to the closed door. "Guys!"

We turned. It was weird, but the smoke inside was being sucked out through the crack underneath it.

"Cool," I said.

"Not so cool," Winona said.

"Backdraft," Joey said. And the way he said it didn't make it sound like a good thing. "We've got to get out of here."

"Sí!" Trashman was already hurrying to the window and opening it. "Vámonos!"

"He's right," Joey said. "Let's go."

Once we got there I looked outside. "It's pretty dark. Where'd everybody go?"

"They're on the other side, genius," Darcy said. "In the parking lot." She turned to Trashman. "You think we can escape this way?"

"Sí, sí! Vámonos! Vámonos!"

She stepped past him and looked down. "Ten feet, no biggie."

We crowded in to see. The grass looked soft enough. And beyond that was a terrace and beyond that, somewhere in the dark, were steps leading to the employee parking lot.

"All right," Darcy said, "I'm in."

We stepped back as she climbed into the window and sat on its ledge.

"Darcy?" I warned.

"What?"

I wasn't sure what to say so I just sort of looked down.

She ran her hand over her bald head. "Well, here goes nothing." She pushed off and fell out of sight. We moved in to see what happened and saw her scramble to her feet. She glanced around, then looked up to us. "No prob," she whispered. "Come on."

"Sí." Trashman sounded more urgent. "Sí, Sí."

"Okay then," Joey said. He climbed into the window. But once his feet were dangling outside, he seemed to have second thoughts.

"Come on," Darcy whispered. "Don't be a wuss."

He nodded, took a breath, and also pushed off. He landed on the grass beside her and then jumped to his feet and looked back up to us. "It's easy," he whispered. "No sweat."

"Come on," Darcy motioned.

Chloe was next. Without any hesitation, she climbed into the window and jumped. Just like that. Then it was Ralphy's turn . . . but not before carefully spreading out his cape for better aerodynamics.

Once he was gone, Winona said, "Let us not forget Max."

"Right!" I said, and me and Nelson went back to the desk and helped him out of the chair.

"Hi, ya, Bernie." He grinned.

"Hi, Max, how are you?"

"Just fine."

"That's great."

When we finally got him to the window and up on the ledge, he looked out into the night, then back to us. "Am I going on a trip?"

"Affirmative," Winona said. "We are vacating this sector."

He grinned. "That's nice."

She called down to the others. "Somebody better catch him."

They all nodded.

She turned to me. "On my count."

Max began to giggle in excitement.

"One, two, three." We pushed him off, and he whooped in excitement as he fell.

When he landed he began laughing, and when they got him to his feet he said, "Again! Let's do it again!"

"Rápido!" Trashman glanced back to the door in concern. "Rápido!"

Nelson went next. "To infinity and beyond!"[33]

And then Winona went.

Now it was just me and Trashman. But when he turned to me, I kinda stepped backward. He frowned like he was confused. Actually, he wasn't the only one. It's not like I was afraid of the jump or anything. It's just, I don't know. I go on field trips all the time. But this . . .

this was leaving for a lot longer. And to be honest, I wasn't sure I liked that.

He must have seen it on my face because his eyes softened like he understood. He reached out his hand to me. I looked down at it, but I couldn't take it.

"Libertad," he said.

I knew exactly what he meant. But I still couldn't take it.

And then, for the first time I could remember, he spoke in English. It was pretty bad because of his accent and everything, but I understood. "Fun," he said.

I understood the word, but I didn't get what he meant.

He tried again. "The hill of grass, it is like."

It took a moment before it dawned on me. "The hill?" I said. "In my dream?"

"Sí . . . in your dream." He motioned again for me to take his hand.

I looked down at it.

"In your dream. Like your dream."

Finally, somehow, I raised my hand and put it into his.

He smiled. "Bien." Then he helped me up into the window. I sat on the edge for a long moment, looking down at the others.

"Come on, Bernie," they whispered. "Let's go, let's go."

I turned to Trashman.

He nodded. "Like your dream."

I scooted closer to the edge. Then, before I could chicken out, he helped me along with a little push. "Adios, amigo."

He was right, it was *EXACTLY* like my dream. There was nothing I could do to stop it. There was no way I could slow down or go back up. I just kept falling. When I finally landed, I crumbled to my knees. But I wasn't hurt. In fact, like Max, I kind of wanted to do it again.

Now there was only Trashman.

"Come on," Joey whispered. "Hurry."

But Trashman was in no hurry. He just stood there smiling down at us.

"Jump," Winona shouted.

"It won't hurt," I said. "I promise."

His smile just grew bigger. Then he called down to us, "Mas archivos."

"What?" Darcy said.

"Mas archivos para destruir."

"He says he has more files to destroy," Ralphy said.

"No," Winona shouted. "You have to jump now!"

But he didn't. Instead, he just reached into his back pocket and pulled out his recorder.

"You've got to jump," Darcy yelled. "It's your only way out." The fact you could see fire in all the other windows said she was probably right.

But instead of jumping, Trashman put his recorder to his mouth and began to play.

"Jump!" We all shouted. "Jump! Jump!"

It was like he didn't hear. He just turned and walked away from the window playing that silly tune—until the room exploded.

A giant fireball roared out the window, shattering the glass into a million pieces that rained down on top of us. Even from where we stood I could feel the heat. And when I looked up, the whole room was blazing.

"No!" Max cried. He tried going for the building and I had to grab him.

"It's okay, Max, it's okay."

But it wasn't okay, and he began sobbing. "No . . . no . . ."

The rest of us just stood there, not believing what had happened. The music had stopped. There was only the sound of hissing wood and crackling fire. And Max's crying.

"Hey!" A voice shouted off to our left. "Are you guys okay?"

We turned to see a couple law enforcement types with flashlights running around the building toward us.

"Is anyone hurt?"

We traded uneasy looks.

"Everyone's meeting in the parking lot on the other side."

Ralphy whispered, "I do not think that is such a good idea."

"Are you patients?" the other called. "If you're patients you need to come with us."

We moved a little closer to each other—maybe even stepped backward a bit.

"Just stay there. We'll come get you."

That's when we all got the same thought at the same time. Joey put it best when he turned to us and calmly shouted, "Run!"

It sounded like a pretty good idea.

thirty

S
A
F
F
R
O
N

JJ got his problems, but one thing you can say 'bout my man, he is smart. Instead of goin' up to the front of the place with its circus of people and flashin' lights, he takes a side street, cuttin' us down behind the woods at the back.

"Less chance a gettin' busted here," he says. And he's right.

We come to a little parkin' lot surrounded by plenty of trees and bushes. I head for the broken down cement steps at the end leadin' up to the building, but JJ stops me. "Too dangerous," he says. "We stay in the woods."

I ain't happy, but a course, he's right. It's tough goin' but we find a little trail and finally get to the top where we just stand starin' at the fire. Pretty impressive and a little scary.

"How we gettin' inside?" I ask.

"We find a way," he says.

We start circlin' 'round, stayin' close to the woods. But it ain't more than a minute 'fore we see half a dozen people runnin' at us. We freeze and pull back into the trees but they seen us. They ain't cops. I'm thinkin' more like EMS, or maybe patients . . . I can't tell. A couple of 'em are half-draggin' some white guy between 'em. When they get to us, a black kid in front shouts, "Where's the stairs?"

A familiar lookin' chick with white hair and aluminum foil wrapped round her neck says, "We are unable to ascertain the appropriate coordinates."

Me and JJ trade looks.

A little Latino guy in goggles and a bath towel steps forward. "Just point the way, and Raphael Montoya Hernandez III shall lead us to freedom."

I got my answer. Definitely not EMS.

The Asian chick, who I also recognize from the soup kitchen, blurts out, "Because you heard the music!"

There's commotion up the terrace toward the building, and we see a couple big guys 'bout a hundred yards away, runnin' our direction. The crazies see 'em too, and we all pull back a little into the woods. The closer they get the more they look like cops so we all stoop down and hide. Jus' 'fore they get to us, they split up—one goin' to our left into the woods, the other to our right.

The bald butch babe which I also remember says, "Where are the stairs?"

"Why should we tell you?" JJ says.

It seems a fair enough question, 'til the big, dough-faced boy who'd insulted me, nods toward the Asian chick and says, "She just told you."

"What?" I say.

"Because you heard the music," he says.

JJ turns to look at me.

I would've said somethin' but I finally recognize who Dough Face is carryin'. It's the dude with them kind eyes. He's all doped up and out of it, but he still manages to spot me and smile. Then he repeats what Dough Face just said. "You heard the music."

I feel a shiver and look away, tryin' to shake it off. But just like them eyes, it don't go away.

"Please," the black kid is sayin', "just show us how to get out of here."

JJ finally nods to the left. "Parkin' lot stairs jus' over there."

They get up from the bushes and start goin' when I hear myself say, "No, they catch you that way for sure."

JJ cuts me a look but I don't care. They ain't bad people, and they ain't competin' with us in the lootin'.

"Where do we go then?" Dough Face asks.

"Not our concern," JJ says. He steps from the bushes toward the building. Of course he expects me to follow and I would, 'cept I get this crazy notion in my head.

Before I can stop, the words tumble out. "Follow me," I say. "There's a path."

JJ death-glares me.

"It'll only take a minute," I say to him. "You go ahead. I be back here in no time."

"Woman . . ." It's as much a threat as a command.

"Hurry." I nod him toward the building. "I'll join you, but you better hurry!"

Before he answers I turn to the woods and start toward the path. The others follow.

"Saffron!"

"Only a minute," I say. "I'll be right back."

He swears some, but I can't hear o'er all the rustlin' bushes and crackin' twigs. I know there be the devil to pay, but I know I need to do this. I ain't sure why, but I know.

"Saffron," Dough Face says. "That's a pretty name."

"Shut up," I say.

He does.

We weave down through the trees and are almost to the parking lot when I hear someone shout, "Over there! I see something!"

"We're busted," the bald woman whispers.

"Not yet," I say. I motion 'em behind the trees. "Get down. Down!"

Everyone starts hidin' 'cept the dude with the kind eyes 'cause I'm grabbin' him from Dough Face. "He stays with me," I say. Dough Face starts to argue but I say louder. "He stays with me." Seein' the concern all over his face, I add a little softer, "Trust me."

A second voice shouts, "I don't see anything."

"Over there!" Flashlight beams dance toward us.

I give Dough Face my best sincere look and he buys it. He let's go the dude, but kneels into the shadows real close, just in case.

The two men are nearly there so I slam Kind Eyes against the nearest tree and start makin' out pretty heavy like he's really gettin' his money's worth. But 'stead of enjoyin' it, he jus' looks at me, so sad and deep-like, that I have to look away. The light hits us and I glance over my shoulder and shout. "Do you mind!"

"What is it?" the second man yells, his beam also findin' us.

"Just some skanky whore."

I swear and yell at 'em to turn off their lights.

"You see anybody else down here?" the first man hollers. "A group of patients, escaped from above?"

"Nothin' down here but customers," I say. "If you boys want some action, you gonna have to wait your turn."

They shake their heads and do some cussin' of their own as they pass us, go into the parkin' lot, and start up the steps. I wait 'til they out of site, all the time not lookin' into the man's eyes. We're only inches apart but I can't look at him.

When it's safe, the others rise from their hidin'.

"That was rather close," the white-haired woman says.

"Where do we go from here?" the black kid says.

No one answers and they all kind of turn toward me.

"How should I know," I say. "Find a hotel, a park. I got business to attend."

"Never fear," the crazy Latino steps forward. "Raphael Montoya Hernandez III shall find the way. Follow me." He heads off the wrong direction and they start to follow.

"Wait a minute," I say. "There ain't nothin' that way."

They stop and turn back to me.

I let go an oath. "You don't know nothin' do you?"

The geek kid with glasses says, "I know Pi rounded to the nearest 40th digit. 3:14159265—"

"Ralphy, shut up," the Butch Babe says.

Ralphy shuts up.

They do more standin'.

I finally sigh. JJ ain't gonna like it, but I don't know what else to do. "Everyone know where the 43B off-ramp is, right?"

No answer.

"Off the 101?"

Still no takers.

"We got a camp there, pretty good size. You can stay there one night, but only one. Clear?"

They nod but keep standing.

"What?" I say.

White Hair answers, "What precisely is a 101?"

I look at their faces. They all equally clueless. I look up the hill to the burnin' building, its orange light flickerin' through the leaves. I turn back to them faces. Pathetic. I s'ppose I could at least start 'em off, point 'em the right direction. "All right." I swear under my breath. "Follow me."

We step out into the parking lot. I ain't happy, I can tell you that. I'm even less happy when I see car lights approach.

"Hide!" I shout.

They scatter back to the woods. Everyone but me. The car don't hit me or nothin', but it slams on its brakes and lays on its horn while slidin' off into tall grass. Course, I return the greeting, both fingers, while shoutin' somethin' 'bout the legitimacy of his birth. But he's too busy tryin' to avoid trees to answer.

And me? I got no idea why I'm doin' what I'm doin'. I only know I should. That don't mean I like it. Only that I should.

thirty-one

D
R

A
A
D
I
L

I sat a moment and took a deep breath. I looked over my shoulder but the woman I'd nearly hit was gone. I took another breath then I dropped the car into reverse and backed through the tall weeds onto the pavement. There was no sign of her or the rest of her group. Most likely the fire had drawn them. The fact they'd disappeared meant they were probably looters come to scavenge whatever they could find.

I shifted into first and drove to my customary parking spot. The main entrance above had been cordoned off for the fire trucks and emergency vehicles. It was a spectacular event. One that I sensed in the pit of my stomach, my patients were somehow major participants.

I turned off the ignition and stepped into the summer night. Even down here the air was filled with the smell of wet charcoal and burning wood. The sight through the trees was surreal.

Up above, the entire structure was ablaze. I started up the crumbling steps leading to the back of the building. The climb was its usual trial but only a precursor to what awaited me.

Once topside I saw there was no chance of saving anything from my office. Even from the distance I could see my window busted out, its surrounding frame scorched black. I kept to the outer perimeter, near the woods, as I rounded to the front of the building.

It was quite the show. Fire trucks, police cars, emergency vehicles, TV trucks and media floodlights. Lots and lots of media floodlights. Scattered here and there were clumps of weeping and terrified patients huddled alongside weeping and terrified staff. There was also the occasional relative who had slipped through the barriers and was calling out for a loved one. All of this amidst the smoke, the fire, the spray, idling trucks, radio chatter, and shouting firemen.

"Dr. Aadil? Dr. Aadil!"

I turned to see Stan Sloan, a bald, portly man, Head of Security. He waddled toward me shouting, "Your patients."

"Pardon me?"

He arrived, panting and wiping his wet face. "Your patients. They're missing."

"What do you mean, *missing*?"

"I mean all the patients are safe and accounted for except those in your pod."

"Which ones?"

"All of them."

I blinked. "That's not possible." He said nothing. "What about Darcy Hamilton in lockup?"

"Unaccounted for."

"Maxwell Portenelli."

"Same."

Bernard Goldstein, surely he's—"

"Doctor, no one from your pod is out here."

"I scanned the lawn, then turned back to the inferno. "They're still inside?"

He shook his head. "Two of our men radioed. They saw half a dozen patients fleeing down the back terrace into the woods."

I stood speechless.

"Doctor!"

I turned to see Alexis Portenelli approach. Her sheer, black dress did little to protect her from the night air, and the unsteady wobble in her heels indicated she'd probably been out partying.

"Where's my father?"

"Good evening, Ms.—"

"Where is he?"

"We're not . . . at this moment, we're uncertain."

She spun to the burning building. "He's still in there!"

Sloan answered, "We don't think so."

She turned back on him. "What do you mean, *YOU DON'T THINK SO?* Don't you know?"

"There's a good possibility he and others in his group have"—he hesitated— "escaped."

"Escaped?"

He nodded.

She searched his face then turned to me. "Because of the transfer?"

I shook my head. "No, that's not possible." But even as I spoke I suspected I was lying. That may be *exactly* why he escaped.

"There's nothing to worry about, Missy." Sloan nodded to the surrounding woods. "We'll find them soon enough."

The girl shivered as we looked into the woods surrounding the building, then turned our gaze down to the city below. Off to our left, the faintest trace of violet had begun rimming the horizon.

She looked back at me, hoping I'd confirm Sloan's statement. I gave no answer, but nodded in silent agreement.

"You've got nothing to worry about," he repeated. "It will all be over shortly. I give you my word. This whole ordeal will be over before you know it."

But even as he spoke, even as I looked out over the city, watching the first signs of life begin to stir, I had my doubts.

With Maxwell Portenelli and his little band of followers, I had some very serious doubts . . .

FOOTNOTE REFERENCES

Chapter Four
  1. California Health and Safety Codes, circa 2054
  2. The NIV Bible, Psalm 145:8

Chapter Nine
  3. Graham Cooke
  4. The King James Bible, Romans 2:4
  5. Ibid. Revelation 12:10

Chapter Eleven
  6. The Declaration of Independence
  7. The King James Bible, 1 John 4:8

Chapter Twelve
  8. Douglas MacArthur
  9. Mary Frances Berry

Chapter Fifteen

10. *Psychology Today,* as quoted in The Possibility Paradigm by Dr. Pamela Gerloff as cited from the blog, Ageing Healthily, Happily, and Youthfully.
11. The NIV Bible, Genesis 2:17
12. Ibid. Psalm 46:10
13. Ibid. Luke 18:17

Chapter Nineteen

14. Benjamin Franklin
15. New King James Bible, John 20:22
16. Ibid. 1 Corinthians 3:16
17. Ibid. Ezekiel 36:27
18. NIV Bible (deity pronouns capitalized), 1 John 4:13
19. Ibid. John 14:20
20. Ibid. John 15:4

Chapter Twenty-one

21. Ibid. NIV Bible, Matthew 22:37
22. Ibid. NIV Bible (deity pronouns capitalized), John 6:57
23. Ibid. NIV Bible, Romans 8:9
24. Ibid. NIV Bible (deity pronouns capitalized), Philippians 2:13

25. Ibid. NIV Bible, Galatians 5:22
26. Ibid. Ibid. John 15:5

Chapter Twenty-three
27. John Fitzgerald Kennedy

Chapter Twenty-four
28. Victor Hugo
29. Confucius
30. NIV Bible, Isaiah 61:1

Chapter Twenty-six
31. William Shakespeare

Chapter Twenty-seven
32. California Statute 55393.2 Circa 2054

Chapter Twenty-nine
33. Buzz Lightyear

Soli Deo gloria

OTHER BOOKS BY BILL MYERS

NOVELS

The Judas Gospel

The God Hater

The Voice

Angel of Wrath

The Wager

Soul Tracker

The Presence

The Seeing

The Face of God

When the Last Leaf Falls

ELI

Blood of Heaven

Threshold

Fire of Heaven

CHILDREN BOOKS

Baseball for Breakfast (picture book)
The Bug Parables (picture book series)
Imager Chronicles (fantasy series)
McGee and Me (book/video series)
The Incredible Worlds of Wally McDoogle (comedy series)
Blood Hounds, Inc. (mystery series)
The Elijah Project (suspense series)
Secret Agent Dingledorf and his trusty dog, Splat (comedy series)
TJ and the Time Stumblers (comedy series)
Truth Seekers (action/comedy series)

TEEN BOOKS

Faith Encounter (devotional)
Hot Topics, Tough Question (non-fiction)
Forbidden Doors (supernatural series)
> *Dark Power Collection*
> *Invisible Terror Collection*
> *Deadly Loyalty Collection*
> *Ancient Forces Collection*

The Dark Side of the Supernatural (non-fiction)

E-BOOK SERIES

Supernatural Love
Supernatural War

For a further list of Bill's books, sample chapters, and
reviews go to www.Billmyers.com
Or check out his Facebook page
www.facebook.com/billmyersauthor

And receive his newsletter announcing the next
installment of
The Last Fool series
by signing up at
http://snipurl.com/billsnews